TIME AFTER TIME

A WITCH IN TIME BOOK 3

****

Jenna St. James

DEDICATION

To the workers in the medical field...thank you for your service.

To Dawn Weigel Miller...may you stay forever young and enjoy your Big Red gum!

Special thanks to Melissa Ann Davison...my wish for you is that every stick of Wrigley's Spearmint gum brings you closer to your Poppy and Gramma.

To all the girls who rocked the Aqua Net...we will always be legends! Especially since the Internet likes to troll and laugh at us.

To Cheryl Standafer...because not only were you fierce with the hair, but you were fearless and knew how to rock a puffy sleeve!

And last but not least...thank you to my family and friends who volunteered to read my first attempt at paranormal writing and who gave me their honest opinions.

Chapter 1

"I'm late!" I snatched my satchel off the filing cabinet and flung it over my shoulder. "I have to go."

"Have fun, Lexi!" Mrs. Carmichael shouted as I ran out of the three-story brick building where I worked.

I glanced across the town square and saw my boyfriend of one month, Shawn Turner, leaning against the wall between BoHo Chic Boutique and The Coffee Bean. Technically, he was leaning against the tall, narrow yellow door that led upstairs to my apartment.

With one more quick wave through the window to Mrs. Carmichael, I hurried down the busy sidewalk, weaving in and out of shoppers. There were thirty active stores on our historic downtown square in River Springs, Missouri, and shoppers were taking advantage of the back-to-school sales.

I'm the assistant curator for the Clay County Historical Society. Not that the county really needed to employ two people to keep up with the little museum—but Mrs. Carmichael had been the curator longer than most of the town council had been alive, and no one had the nerve to demand she retire.

Being the assistant curator was my day job. It kept me busy and helped me brush up on history. I actually have another job...a *real* job. One that I take very seriously. For a little over a year now, I've worked for the Agency of Paranormal Peculiarities as a time-traveling, cold-case solving witch.

To most people, I was Lexi Catherine Sanders...fiercely independent, smart, sassy, and sometimes funny. However, when I'm on the job to solve a cold case, I always use my mom's family name of Howe. I come from a long line of witches. My too-many-greats-to-count grandmother was tried and convicted for being a witch during the Salem Witch Trials.

All the women in my family have certain abilities that come naturally to them. For me, it was movement. I have the ability to move objects up to six feet in any direction. Plus, if I concentrate just right, I can "sense" people who are not immediately in front of me. Not their names per say, more like I can sense where they are in my surrounding area. A pretty good perk when you need to snoop.

Using my magical abilities and an enchanted spell given to me by the Agency of Paranormal Peculiarities, I can travel back in time and solve crimes that were never solved by the police. It was an amazing rush every time I jumped back in time. Of course, my biggest fear was one day I'd have to travel back to the nineteen sixties when miniskirts were the fad. I just didn't have the legs to pull that off.

I spend a lot of time cramming and learning about different time periods so I'd be better prepared on jobs. But it seemed no matter how much I read and brushed up on current events, I was always a little bit of a fish out of water while on assignment. Luckily, I'd been given a familiar—a magical creature in the form of an animal—on every cold case I'd worked thus far, so I had help when I needed it. During my last assignment, I'd had a beautiful long-haired Birman cat to help show me the way.

I jogged across the small crosswalk and waved to Shawn. He grinned and pushed away from the door, his muscular body hidden beneath the suit he wore.

"Hey, Lexi." He leaned down and brushed his lips across my cheek.

Shawn Turner was everything I wanted in a guy—which was exactly why I needed to keep him at arm's length. He was in his early thirties, nearly six feet tall, light brown hair, hazel eyes, easy smile, and with his toned body, he was a sight to behold. But when you added the sharp mind of a lawyer and the strange ability to see through all my defenses, it put me on guard during most of our dates.

I normally dated guys superficially. A date here, a date there. Never anything serious. But Shawn wasn't having any of my aloof, sometimes manipulative ways. On more than one occasion he'd called me on my behavior. It seemed the more I tried to push him away...the more he didn't budge.

"I'm so sorry." I unlocked the wooden door and pushed it open. The smell of lavender and peppermint greeted me. "I lost track of time." I turned on the light switch and started up the fifteen steps that led to my apartment. Fifteen steep, exhausting steps. It was the only downside to my fabulous, eight hundred square foot abode.

At the top of the stairs, a tiny hallway led straight back to the kitchen. Immediately to the right of the stairs was my living room/bedroom, with the bathroom centered in the tiny hallway just before you reached the kitchen.

"No hurry," Shawn said. "We still have an hour before we need to be at the winery."

Usually we eat at one of the many restaurants on the historic downtown square. But tonight Shawn wanted to go to Gravestone Winery, a local establishment that had opened a month ago. Back in the eighteen hundreds it had been called Gravestone Asylum. The building had started out as an insane asylum and had continued to be a mental hospital up until nineteen seventy-six, when something happened that caused the facility to close. The building was then sold, and in nineteen eighty-five it reopened as a small, privately owned assisted living facility. Unfortunately, the assisted living facility closed by nineteen ninety-five. Some locals around town believed the building was cursed, while others claimed the place was haunted.

I'd driven by the monstrous winery a couple times, and I had to admit, it was an imposing sight. Especially with the graveyard in the back.

"Just give me a minute to change." I steered Shawn into the living room that also doubled as my bedroom.

"Here." I shoved a book at him and pushed him down on the couch. "You can do a little light reading while I get ready."

Shawn glanced down at the book in his hand and raised an eyebrow. "Seriously, Lexi? *The Art of War* by Sun Tzu is your idea of light reading?"

I snorted at his dry tone. "Just hush up and read it."

I'd been given the suggestion to read the military treatise by my friend and fellow cold-case solving witch, Nuala Walsh. She was as dedicated and systematic as they come. I thought of her more like a ninja than a witch.

Shawn settled back into the sofa and opened the book. I hurried behind the partition where I kept my clothes and grabbed my favorite summer dress off the hanger. Running to the bathroom, I slid to a stop in front of the one-hundred-year-old door. I turned the knob and pushed. Nothing. The darned thing was so old and heavy that most days it didn't want to open. Not without an exhausting fight anyway. Gripping the handle tightly, I hit the door with both my hip and my shoulder.

It still didn't budge.

Looking over my shoulder to make sure Shawn couldn't see me from inside the living room, I waved my hand in front of the door. It slid open like butter on hot pancakes.

I was on a roll. Nothing could stop me now.

Thump!

My heart lurched at the sound. I knew that sound!

No, no, no, no, no.

I threw my dress inside the bathroom and took off for the kitchen. Since it was only three steps away from the living room/bedroom and bathroom...it didn't take long.

I hurried over to the narrow kitchen door and stepped out onto the rickety balcony. It was a twelve-foot drop down to the ground. There was no staircase, just a wobbly old fire escape that I prayed I'd never have to use. There was no way a box should be sitting on the balcony.

But there it was.

Scowling, I grabbed the box and ran back inside. Cursing my bad luck the whole way to the bathroom.

"Everything okay?" Shawn asked as he leaned against the door jamb to the bathroom.

8

I screamed and tried to shove the box behind me...but it was too big.

"Whatcha got there?" Shawn asked.

"Nothing. Just something I found on the balcony."

Shawn frowned and looked behind me. "On the balcony? How'd it get there?"

"I put it there."

"What?" Shawn reached up and tucked a curl behind my ear. "You feeling okay, Lexi?"

"Yep. Couldn't be better."

Think! Think!

"I'm almost ready," I babbled. "I just need a few more minutes."

"You look beautiful," Shawn said. "You don't need to—"

I pushed against his chest. "I need to shave my legs!"

"What?"

Shut up, Lexi!

"Um...I need to shave my legs. You know, it's a special date. Our one-month anniversary and all."

The corner of Shawn's mouth lifted in a smile. "Lexi, I'm not expecting—"

"I forgot to shave my legs!"

Stop screaming at the man!

"I heard you," Shawn said, speaking to me in a slow, soothing voice. "But just so we're clear, I'm not expecting—"

"Go! I won't be but a minute!"

Shawn shook his head, turned around, and walked back toward the living room. Breathing a sigh of relief, I hurried into the bathroom, slammed the door behind me, and rested my head against the door.

You can do this, Lexi!

I glanced down at the box still in my hands and scowled at the stupid thing...but the box didn't seem to care. Knowing I couldn't put it off any longer, I sat down on the edge of my clawfoot tub, placed the box on the floor, and pried off the lid.

The first item I pulled out was a pair of acid-washed jeans. They looked four sizes too big. The jeans had eight buttons in the front, a tag that read Z. Cavaricci, and more pleats than a schoolgirl's uniform. I stood and held them to me. The waistband reached my boobs. I'd read about the high-rise jeans of the 80s, but this was ridiculous!

Next item was a cobalt blue Guess sweatshirt. It, too, looked four sizes too big. A pair of scrunchy white socks and white Sperry shoes with a blue stripe around the top, and the largest pair of hooped earrings I'd ever seen in my life finished off the ensemble.

I stripped off my clothes and pulled on the jeans. I'd been right. The waistband hit just under my bra. There's no way women seriously wore these things. I picked up my phone and Googled Z. Cavaricci jeans. I breathed a sigh of relief when I saw a picture of a girl in my exact jeans with the top four buttons opened and splayed apart. I quickly unbuttoned the jeans and pressed them flat. Or as flat as I could get them considering I had an extra poof of gathered material over my stomach. Who the heck thought pleats were flattering?

It didn't take but a couple minutes to finish putting on the rest of the clothes. Stepping in front of the mirror I barely held in a scream. I didn't look like a twenty-five-year-old modern witch...I looked like a monochromatic blue blob. But at least it wasn't the stirrup pants with high heels and bright tops I remember my mom saying she wore.

Why hadn't I paid more attention to her when she talked non-stop about growing up in the 80s? If I had more time—and if I knew exactly where she was—I'd reach out and call her. Mom was a jet setter. One week she could be in Cairo, the next week in Tuscany. Usually, I'd get a text with some vague destination. I loved my mom, but she was a hard witch to pin down.

I picked up the manila file folder at the bottom of the box and quickly flipped through. To my astonishment, there wasn't much to go on. A yellowed newspaper clipping with the date August 15, 1988 reported two deaths in one week at a nursing home. The head nurse, Margaret Noland, fell to her death, while nursing home resident, Paul Ridgeway, died of natural causes. However, staff, residents, and even community members believed the building to be cursed and haunted.

That was it. No location, no suspects...nothing.

Another typewritten note from the Agency of Paranormal Peculiarities informed me that while the police department officially closed the case saying there was no connection between the two deaths, the detective in charge, Ryan Hackett, had always maintained there was more to the story.

"That's it?" I cried in exasperation as I slammed the folder shut.

A knock sounded on the door. "Lexi? You about done? We really need to think about going."

"One more minute!"

On every cold case assignment I'd had so far, I'd received a handful of tools. Things that might aide me in my investigation. I bent down and grabbed the rest of the items out of the box. A cassette labeled "80s mixed tape," two quarters, a miniature can of Aqua Net hair spray, and a package of Wrigley's Big Red gum.

"What the heck?" I shoved my tools in the front pocket of my spacious, baggy jeans. No surprise...everything fit, and I had room for more. "This is the *worst* box so far."

I mean, it wasn't like I didn't know what time period I was traveling to. I just couldn't figure out what all the clues meant. I got the quarters. No cell phones during that time, so I'd need a quarter if I needed to call someone. But a cassette tape? A package of gum? And hair spray? What did it all mean?

And what exactly did I know about the 80s? Colorful, loose clothing, quirky way of talking, and decent music. I had no idea about current events, television shows, movies—well, except for a couple movies. And that's only because my fellow time-traveling, cold-case solving friend, Mariana Galvin, had invited us all over to her house one night for an 80s party. She was the only one of us five witches who'd been a teenager during that time, so we figured it would be fun. She'd met us at her door and made us all don neon green leg warmers and matching neon green fishnet gloves. We'd drank Bartles & Jaymes wine coolers and watched *Lost Boys*, *The Breakfast Club*, *Footloose*, and *Sixteen Candles*.

So basically my understanding of the 80s after that night was that people feared vampires, Molly Ringwald gave diamond earrings to boys she liked, dancing was banned in some towns, Jake Ryan was the man, and after eight Bartles & Jaymes wine coolers, I was still stone-cold sober.

Another knock. "Are you sure you're okay in there?"

I hurried to the door, then at the last minute remembered how I was dressed. Hiding behind the door, I cracked it open. "I had a small accident with my shaver. No biggie. But I'm going to need a few more minutes, okay?"

"Do you need help?"

"Nope. I just need time. Give me ten minutes?"

In truth, I didn't feel too badly about making him wait. When I traveled back from where I was going, I would return back to right now at this time in this bathroom. So it's not like he'd be waiting forever on me.

Shawn winked at me. "Sure thing, Lexi."

"Thanks."

I slammed the door in his face and ran to my bathroom cabinet. I yanked out a small box and set it on the bathroom floor before plunking down beside it.

Opening the box, I carefully withdrew the black tourmaline necklace inside. My mother had the necklace commissioned for me when I started my job with the Agency of Paranormal Peculiarities. Black tourmaline was said to be one of the most powerful protection stones around. I only wear it during my time-travel jobs.

I dropped the necklace over my head and drew in a deep breath before slowly letting it out. I knew the spell I needed to say by heart. I was free to write it down and then burn the paper as I said it, but I preferred to picture the words in my head as I said the spell aloud.

Taking another deep breath, I held it, and then slowly let it out. Seeing the words I'd need to not only propel myself through time, but to also make sure I didn't cause a ripple of any kind...I centered myself. I pushed out all the noise and chaos around me, closed my eyes, and focused on my job at hand.

When I felt the time was right, I started the spell:

"Crimes are unpunished
The world's not right.
Cosmos guide me into the time-travel light.
To the past I'll travel
Absent of any time ripple.
Nineteen eighty-eight is my time
To solve this heinous crime."

CHAPTER 2

I slowly opened my eyes and took in my surroundings. Or at least I tried to take in my surroundings. A massive, overgrown green bush inches from my face kept me from enjoying the view. Well, that plus the fact jumping through time often left me feeling shaky and nauseated.

I pushed the hedge aside and staggered around to the front of the building. A set of five cement steps led up to the front of the monstrous structure. I was surprised to see a black and white police car parked in the mile-wide circular driveway.

I took a couple steps back so I could get a better view. A sidewalk approximately six feet by twenty feet ran to the front door straight off the cement steps, and colossal stone pillars stood on each side of the twelve-foot door. The sprawling, two-story stone structure reminded me of an old British palace. Even though there was a spooky element to the place, there was no denying it was magnificent.

I frowned.

There was something vaguely familiar about the building. Heading toward the steps, I spotted an old metal sign nestled in the mulch. I squinted and tried to make out the rusted letters.

I gasped when I finally realized what it said: Hospital of the Insane.

"No way! Gravestone Winery?"

Only it wasn't the modern-day winery I'd seen on my recent drive-bys...it was the insane asylum! My heart started to beat double time, and I was about to hyperventilate when

I remembered I was in the 80s. By this time Gravestone Asylum had been turned into a privately-owned assisted living facility.

Stay calm, Lexi!

Usually I wasn't the type of witch who scared easily, but the thought of spending the night in an insane asylum set me on edge a little more than I cared to admit. It was times like this I needed my best friend and fellow cold-case solving witch, Vee Harper. She loved fighting shifters and things that went bump in the night.

A sudden gust of wind snapped my neck to the right.

What the heck? Since when didn't the wind blow through my hair?

I reached up, patted my hair, and almost screamed in fright. My bangs were standing practically two feet in the air. Running my hands down the rest of my usually silken mane, I whimpered at the wings sticking out at my temples. Pulling the ends of my hair in front of me, I marveled at the tight curls.

A perm! An actual fry-your-hair 80s perm!

"Deep breath, Lexi. It's only until you solve this case."

I cursed when I felt something sharp slice across the canvas of my shoe. I glanced down and stifled a groan. Peering up at me through black beady eyes was a huge gray rat. He was standing up on his hind legs, pink paws twitching nervously.

I sighed. Just my luck, my familiar for the case would be a rat. Not that I had anything against rats, it's just they had a tendency to suffer from major ADHD and talked a mile a minute.

16

Hello. Hello. Name's Rex. Rex the Rat. That's what my friends call me. Rex the Rat. I'm here for you. Just ask, and I'll do.

I scooped Rex up and held him close to my chest.

"Hello, Rex. My name's Lexi."

Lexi? Lexi, you say? Okay. Okay. I can remember that. Yes. Yes, I can. Lexi. Lexi. Lexi.

I was getting a headache, and I hadn't even made it inside the building. I tucked Rex in my *other* spacious front pocket and carefully made my way up the cement stairs. At the top of the landing, a silver-encased payphone sat to the left of the staircase. I ran my hand over the cool metal. Glad to know I was right about the quarters.

I turned toward the massive front door and nearly stroked out when I saw a lone figure leaning against the side of the stone building. How had I missed him? Oh, that's right. Because my brain had nearly exploded at the thought that I'd have to stay the night in an insane asylum.

The guy stared at me as he puffed away on his cigarette. I glanced over my shoulder to make sure he couldn't have witnessed my sudden appearance out of nowhere or seen me talking to a rat. That might leave me with a lot of explaining to do.

I put him in his early twenties. He was dressed in all white as he leaned against the wall. His frizzy, blond hair was cut short in the front and sides, but in the back it reached his shoulders.

A mullet. I recognized it from the movie *Joe Dirt.*

"Dude, like, where'd you come from?" He motioned to me with his cigarette. "You here to apply for one of the job openings as an aide?"

"Yes," I said, grasping at straws.

Mullet Boy snorted, pulled on his cigarette again, and scanned the yard once more. I caught just the slightest hint of fear in his eyes. "Why'd you want to do that? Everyone else is running from here. This place is haunted. Haven't you heard we're cursed?"

"No."

A baby sneeze erupted from my jean's pocket, and I barely resisted the urge to slap my hand down over the rat.

"What was that?" Mullet Boy asked, his eyes going wide.

"I didn't hear anything," I lied.

Bless me! Bless me!

"You didn't hear that?" Mullet Boy whimpered. "It sounded like someone behind you sneezed."

I made a dramatic show of looking over my shoulder before turning back to him. "I don't see anyone."

"See what I mean? We're haunted." Mullet Boy took another drag.

"I'm not afraid," I insisted.

Mullet Boy nodded as though he felt the same way. "That's cool." But the slight tremble in his hands as he smoked told me he was lying, and his constant scanning of the grounds unnerved me.

He flicked his cigarette away and pushed himself off the wall. It was all I could do not to flick *him* upside the head. Didn't he know about littering? Not to mention he could start a fire.

18

The front door opened, and two plainclothes detectives walked out. They were complete opposites—from their build, to their age, to their style of dress. They stopped when they saw us.

"I believe I've spoken with you," the older detective said to Mullet Boy. "But not you. Do you work here?"

I pointed to myself. "Me? Not yet. But I hope to be employed here shortly."

The older detective narrowed his eyes. He was middle aged, slightly paunchy around the stomach, had a bad combover, and if I had to guess by his wrinkled slacks and shirt, I'd say he didn't own an iron...but his eyes were clear and sharp. Definitely a seasoned detective.

Unlike the unusually young detective next to him. He was tall, mid-twenties, athletic, handsome, and his standard-issue white shirt and black tie combination were clean and crisp.

The older detective handed me a card. "My name's Detective Hackett, and this is my partner Detective Seaver. And let me just warn you, little lady, you might want to rethink employment here. There's been a round of bad luck lately at the nursing home. I'm here today asking follow-up questions regarding the deaths of Nurse Margaret Noland and resident Paul Ridgeway."

I took his card, glanced down at it, then stuck out my hand. "Lexi Howe. New in town and still looking for a job regardless."

"I told her she was crazy to come here," Mullet Boy said. "People are saying this place is haunted. It's been cursed."

I shrugged and kept my eyes on Detective Hackett. "And I informed him curses and haunted places don't scare me."

"Is that so?" Detective Hackett gave me a hard stare. "Well, if you do happen to retain employment here at Gravestone Manor, and you come across anything you think I need to know about regarding the deaths of either Nurse Margaret Noland or Paul Ridgeway, please don't hesitate to call."

"Dude," Mullet Boy said, "I'm telling you, Pauley died from natural causes. The guy'd already had one stroke six months ago. It's not like his death was a shock."

Detective Hackett gave Mullet Boy a tight smile. "That's what everyone keeps telling me. Well, everyone but one person."

Mullet Boy rolled his eyes. "Mac."

"Good day, Ms. Howe." Detective Hackett turned on his heel and continued down the sidewalk and steps toward his police car.

"Have a good day," Detective Seaver echoed as he followed after his partner.

"Guy's wasting his time," Mullet Boy muttered. He turned and pushed opened the front door. Grinning, he gestured for me to enter. "After you."

While I didn't get a sinister vibe from this guy, there was something about him that put me off. I didn't know if it was because he was being a jerk, or if it was because deep down he was scared. And just because I could, I concentrated on the door and slammed it shut before Mullet Boy could physically close it.

"Oh, man," he whimpered. "Did you see that? This place really *is* haunted."

CHAPTER 3

"You got a name?" I asked.

I didn't want to call him Mullet Boy during my entire time here.

He laughed nervously, still looking around to see how the door closed. "Billy."

The inside of the building was a complete surprise. The floor sparkled and gleamed, there was a fresh, clean smell in the air, and overall the interior had a homey feel. Not what I expected from a former insane asylum.

Immediately to my left was an open set of stone steps leading downstairs to the basement. Unlike the bright whiteness of the first floor, what I could see of the basement looked gloomy and sinister. I'd obviously spoken too soon about the overall homey feel.

"Of course there's a dark, creepy asylum basement," I muttered to myself. "Wouldn't expect anything less."

Don't be a scaredy witch! I ain't afraid. They don't call me Rex the Brave for nothing.

"Watch it, rat," I hissed.

Across the hall was a spacious nurses station, and on either side of the station were hallways leading off to other parts of the nursing home.

As Billy and I made our way to the nurses station, I noticed there was a set of stairs to my right that led up to the second floor.

"This is Nurse Lohman," Billy said. "She's the nurse in charge during the morning shift."

A short, stocky bulldog of a woman turned from the filing cabinet, a bundle of folders in her arms. She was dressed in a white, knee-length uniform with a white hat in her hair.

"My name's Lexi Howe," I said. "I'm here to apply for a job as an aide."

Nurse Lohman ran her eyes up and down me. "I don't think this is your kind of job."

Do I seriously look that *incompetent?*

My jean pocket started to move. *The curse, the curse! Mention the curse! Two deaths in one week!*

"I know about the curse," I said. "Do you really think anyone else is going to apply?"

Nurse Lohman's eyes snapped back to me. "What did you say?"

Billy laughed nervously, and I saw the fear again in his eyes.

"Plus, I just met two of your city's finest outside," I continued, "I don't think you're gonna have people beating down the door to get inside after two deaths in one week *and* cops hanging around a workplace."

"Nurse Noland's death was an accident," Nurse Lohman snapped. "She was going downstairs for medication. She slipped and fell. As for the death of Paul Ridgeway...residents die. All proper procedures were followed immediately upon his death."

"Really? And the curse that's been placed on the facility? How do you explain that? Curses don't just go away, you know?"

"You know about curses?" Billy asked.

"I know a thing or two about them," I said cryptically. "Especially casting them when I'm angry."

Billy gasped and looked terrified. I almost felt like a heel for what I was about to do next.

Almost.

But I had a job to do. I had to solve a cold-case murder, and I couldn't let my feelings get in the way. Especially when, for all I knew, one of these two could be involved.

"I also know about hauntings. I bet crazy things happen all the time? Right?" I gestured to a pen lying on the counter. "Like I bet that pen right there might just roll off the counter and fall to the floor."

I concentrated on the pen and smiled inside when it rolled to the edge of the counter and fell on the floor. Billy let out a little shriek and jumped backward. Even the stalwart Nurse Lohman looked shaken.

I bent down to pick up the pen off the floor.

Nurse Lohman shoved a clipboard at me. "Fill out the application. I'll need you to list references. Usually if a new hire comes in, Dr. Stark sees to the hiring. But since we are so short-staffed, I've been given the go-ahead to do the hiring. If everything pans out, when can you start?"

"Immediately," I said.

"Will you live on grounds or commute?" Nurse Lohman asked.

"Excuse me?" I asked.

"All workers have the choice to live on the second floor or commute. The second floor is gated and locked at all times. Only workers are allowed up there."

24

I sighed. It looked like I'd be spending the night in an insane asylum anyway. I didn't have the finances or transportation to look for a place to stay.

"I'll stay on the second floor," I grumbled.

"Fine. We are a privately-owned nursing home with about twenty beds right now. In fact, it's not even really a nursing home. Not how you might think. Nearly all the residents here are self-sufficient and just need minimal care and attention." Nurse Lohman turned to Billy. "Go find her a room."

"Me?" Billy squeaked, still gawking at me like I'd grown an extra head. "Why me?"

"You will start on the evening shift since they are the shortest staffed," Nurse Lohman said, ignoring Billy's question. "You will work from three to midnight. You get an hour for lunch. You may either eat in the lounge down here on this floor, upstairs in the remodeled lounge, or your personal room."

Nurse Lohman walked over to a metal cabinet, looked me up and down again, reached inside, and withdrew two white uniforms. She marched back over and thrust the pile at me. "Do you have proper undergarments?"

I blanched. "Excuse me?"

Nurse Lohman sighed. "Do you have white support hose?"

Support hose? Like nylons?

Ohhh la la! Sexy!

"No," I said, doing my best to ignore the rat fink inside my pocket. "I guess not."

Nurse Lohman sighed again, walked back to the cabinet, and pulled out a package. She then marched back over and slammed them on top of the uniform.

"Put her in one of the vacant rooms," Nurse Lohman said. "Do *not* put her in Nurse Noland's old room. There's plenty to choose from now that word is out of what's happened here."

I followed Billy up the first set of stairs. At the top of the landing in between the first and second floor, we turned and headed up the last of the stairs that would take us to the second floor. At the top of the stairs he pulled out a key and unlocked the metal, black gate.

"It's pretty silent up here now," Billy said. "We've had over half our staff quit in the last two days. Two deaths in one week hasn't been good for business...even though, like Nurse Lohman said, one was an accident and the other old age. But people are superstitious, I suppose."

"I suppose so," I agreed. "How empty is it up here?"

The hallway upstairs, like the hallway downstairs, split into two sections. Like an east wing and a west wing in a fancy house. But unlike the downstairs, the second floor was in deplorable shape. I'd say all the money had been spent on the renovations of the first floor.

"Very empty," Billy said. "Like three or four people. Do you really know a lot about curses and stuff?"

"Yep."

Billy went to shut and lock the gate, but before he could, I waved my hand and the gate slammed shut with a loud clang.

Billy whimpered and quickly bent to lock up.

26

The stone-walled hallway split to the left and right, each hallway about thirty feet long. I quickly counted five doors down and five doors across, for a total of ten rooms on each wing of the hallway.

Billy gestured to the left. "About three years ago when they made this place into a nursing home, they knocked down a wall and made two bedrooms into one big kitchen and living room area. It's the last door on the right at the end of this hall. There's a refrigerator in there, too. Just label your food and it should be okay. The only rule is you clean up what you dirty."

We turned right and headed down the cold, narrow corridor away from the kitchen. The only overhead light was a drop-down bulb that swayed back and forth, causing the chain to squeak. A large, oversized laundry cart was parked in the middle of the hallway.

"There's a laundry room across from where you are staying," Billy said. "You can probably just carry your clothes and bedding over. The others usually need carts. Or they did when people stayed up here."

"So most of these rooms are empty now?" I asked.

"Yep. Like I said, I think only four rooms are now occupied on this floor. A total of three people have quit so far, and two of them lived up here."

"How do you run the place on such a short staff?" I asked.

Billy shrugged. "It's really not that bad. Like Nurse Lohman said, this is a small facility of about twenty or so residents, and the old people here are great. For the most part, they just need a little extra care. They aren't like the people you see in other nursing homes. Most of these guys are pretty self-sufficient. They take pride in that."

"So who's up here now?"

"The head nurse and aide on your night shift tonight, Nurse Shue and Stew Rodgers, they still live up here. Nurse Noland used to live up here, too." Billy bit his lip. "But not anymore, obviously. Everyone else either quit or are now commuting. They don't want to stay up here no more. Oh, and on the graveyard shift, there's a guy who lives up here. He's an aide. But he keeps to himself. Graveyard shift only works from midnight to six, and there's only one head nurse and two aides for those six hours. Well, one aide now that Judy quit. But she always commuted anyway."

"Cozy." So that made about three people by my count...four including me. "You don't stay up here?"

Billy blushed. "Nah. I got me a girlfriend. I crash at her place."

We stopped in front of a door that looked identical to the others. He bent down and used a key to open it, gesturing for me to go through. I wanted to joke to him that I'd stayed in worse places...but I really hadn't.

Billy swallowed, his Adam's apple bobbing nervously up and down. "This is your room. I'll be back in a little while to get your paperwork."

Without waiting for my response, Billy turned and fled out of the room.

"Was it something I said?" I deadpanned as I took Rex out of my pocket.

The rat squeaked and bobbed his head up and down. I took that to mean he was laughing at my comment.

28

"Do me a favor, Rex, and go figure out the lay of the land. See where the rooms are, who the people are, that kind of thing." I rolled my eyes in disgust. "I mean, seeing as how Billy just left and didn't leave me a key. And now I'm basically *trapped* up here."

You betcha, Lexi!

Chapter 4

Thirty sweaty minutes later I was dressed in a pristine white dress that cinched in at the waist, fell to my knees, and had two huge pockets on the front. I was a freakin' sweaty mess because it took twenty minutes for me to wiggle and jiggle my plump butt into the support hose I'd been given. I thought wrestling into a Spanx was rough...it had *nothing* on support hose!

I looked down at my ridiculous outfit—white nylons with Sperry shoes—and tried not to cry. I hadn't felt this ridiculous on an assignment in a long time.

I gathered up the clipboard and sat down on the cold, hard cot to fill out the employment papers. The room was surprisingly spacious. Unfortunately, the only furniture in it was the twin-sized cot, a rickety old desk, and an antique chair so ancient I was afraid I'd fall through if I sat on it.

The only positive thing I saw was the room had been remodeled about fifty years ago. So instead of broken stone walls, I had cracked and marred plaster walls that were a peachy, salmon color. All in all, I figured if I had to stay more than a week in here, I'd seriously go crazy.

A knock sounded on my bedroom door, and I was half tempted to wave my hand and open it. But I didn't want poor Billy to die of fright. Sighing, I set the paperwork down on the bed and walked over to open the door.

"Dude, Nurse Lohman sent me up here. Are you finished with the paperwork? She said to tell you that you can start tonight at six since you're probably still getting settled in. She'll leave Nurse Shue a note to tell her about you." He handed me a keychain with two keys. "Keep this on you at all times. One key fits the gate, the other your room."

"Thanks," I said and grabbed the keys from him.

There was no need for me to have a key to my room. I'd already cast a protection spell around my door so that the only people who could enter freely were Rex and me. If someone tried to break in, they'd get a little zap from an energy bolt.

"I'm almost finished," I said, "but I'm having a hard time thinking of three references."

In truth, I had no idea what to do. I didn't know three people in this time period that could vouch for me.

"Just do what I did," Billy said. "Put in your parents and friends."

Oh, boy! Forgive me, Mom.

"Both of my parents have passed on," I lied. "And I just moved to town, so I don't really know anyone."

Billy frowned...then perked up. "Hey, I know! Like, how about I give you names? You can put down my mom's phone number. I'll run outside to the payphone and tell her what's going on, and that her secret name today is Pam. She'll do it for us. She's cool like that."

I almost felt ashamed for calling him Mullet Boy and scaring him half to death.

"That's real nice of you," I said.

I slid a quarter off my desk and handed it to Billy.

"You seem like a cool chick." He pocketed the quarter. "A little strange, but cool."

"Do you know of anyone else who'd vouch for me?" I asked.

31

"I'll call my girlfriend Heather. Tell her to pretend to be my aunt who works at a hospital in Kansas City. Her name's Janet if you want to put that name down."

"I only have one more quarter to my name," I said. "Will you need it, too?"

Billy chuckled. "Nah. It's cool, dude. It used to be I'd hack the phone outside using the method Matthew Broderick used in *War Games*, but now when I call Heather on my breaks, I just call collect and say what I need to real quick. When the operator asks for my name today, I'll say, 'Pretend you're Janet today.' This way I won't have to pay for the call. And Heather'll be cool with it. She won't ask questions. I can't really do that with my mom, that's why I'd need the quarter for her."

I had absolutely no idea what he was talking about, but I nodded anyway and scribbled down Billy's mom's information, along with Heather-Janet's name and a phone number.

"That should be enough," Billy said. "We got tons of openings right now. Nurse Lohman was just trying to scare you. She ain't really gonna call all these people."

Billy picked up my cassette off the desk. "What songs are on here?"

I shrugged. "I don't know."

He gave me a strange look.

"I mean, I did it so long ago," I said, "that I've forgotten."

"Cool. There's a boombox in the rec room. I bet you can play it down there if you want."

"Thanks, I just might."

32

"I'll be finished with my shift before you start," Billy said. "So word of advice, don't let Mac drive you too crazy."

Before I could ask who Mac was, Billy walked out of the room with my paperwork.

I leaned back against the crumbling wall and thought about what I knew so far. In one week's time, two deaths had occurred at Gravestone Manor. While that was unusual, I wasn't sure why some of the staff automatically assumed it was a curse or that the place was haunted and not something more nefarious.

"It's funny, isn't it, the kind of stuff that pops into your head when you're trying to work?"

I blinked at the petite old man who'd suddenly appeared in the doorway, talking to me like I knew who he was. He couldn't have been more than five feet tall, maybe one hundred pounds soaking wet, bald, and sporting more wrinkles than a Shar-Pei. He had on brown pants with a white uniform jacket like Billy's. Only his looked like it was about to swallow him whole it was so big.

"Excuse me?" I asked.

"I said it's funny, you know, the kind of stuff that pops into your head when you're trying to work. I remember this one time my father took me to a circus to see a horse show. I watched the horse prance around the arena, and I thought to myself, I'm going to ride that horse. Of course, I really didn't know—"

"I don't mean to be rude," I said as kindly as I could. "But can I help you?"

I knew he had to be another employee if he was on the second floor and dressed in a uniformed jacket.

"Oh, I'm sorry. Name's Mac. Angus MacGyver, actually. But my friends all call me Mac."

"So *you're* Mac," I said. "My name's Lexi."

"Lexi? That's not a name you hear every day."

Just you wait.

"Well, Mac, I've heard a lot about you."

He put his finger over his lips, looked behind him, then hurried the rest of the way into my room. "I'm keeping a low profile while I'm here."

"Don't want to be at work, huh? I get it."

Mac quirked his eyebrow. "I need to keep a low profile because of who I am."

"Whaddya mean?" I asked.

"Let's just say, when there's a problem, the company I work for, the Phoenix Foundation, sends me in to troubleshoot and save the day."

"Is the Phoenix Foundation the name of the company that sends out nurses or something?"

"No."

"What's your specialty?" I asked.

"Well, I once stopped a bomb with a paperclip."

I laughed. "What?"

Mac nodded solemnly. "I'm very resourceful."

"How long have you worked here?"

Mac furrowed his brow. "Awhile now. I usually have my trusty Swiss Army knife and duct tape on me. I can build anything as long as I have duct tape."

He must be in maintenance and not nursing.

"So you're like a fix-it man," I said. "Where's your duct tape now?"

34

Mac frowned. "The night nurse in charge now, her name's Nurse Shue. She took it from me. She used to not care that I had them, but now she's all by-the-book and keeps getting mad. I guess maybe because her best friend was one of the people that died last week."

I perked up. "Nurse Shue's friend? You mean Nurse Noland that died?"

"That's what I said."

"Start at the beginning, Mac. The nurse that died, what was her name?"

"Nurse Noland," Mac said. "I liked her. She never took my duct tape or knife away. She would tell me she understood why I needed them. Nurse Shue was the same way. But now if Nurse Shue sees them, she takes them away." He grinned. "But I always manage to get them back."

"How did Nurse Noland die?" I asked, trying to keep him focused.

Mac shrugged. "She broke her neck. some people say she fell down the stairs, while others say she was pushed by a ghost."

"So Nurse Noland was the head night nurse until she died last week. And now her best friend, Nurse Shue, is the head nurse?"

Mac nodded. "And each day she's getting meaner and meaner."

"Nurse Shue is? Well, she's probably stressed from all that's going on."

Stressed from killing her best friend for her job position. Sounds like a nice motive to me.

"Stew is happy, though," Mac said. "He hated Nurse Noland."

Something told me this Mac guy and Rex could be great friends. Neither one of them could stay on a topic long.

"I've heard Stew's name before," I said. "Who's he?"

"Stew? He works the night shift. He's really mean. Nurse Noland didn't like him at all. She wrote him up twice. He's not always nice to the old people, and he's got a bad temper."

"You're kidding?"

"Nurse Noland told him right before she died that if she wrote him up one more time he was fired!" Mac grinned. "We all clapped."

So my suspects now are best friend Nurse Shue and Abuser Stew. Great, now I was rhyming everything like Rex the Rat.

"Anyone else who might want to hurt Nurse Noland?" I asked.

Mac shook his head. "Oh, no. Everyone else here loved her." He leaned forward and wiggled his eyebrows. "Even Dr. Stark. He comes in every morning and every evening to do his rounds. Makes sure everyone is doing well. A few months ago I caught him and Nurse Noland kissing. But they made me swear I wouldn't tell anyone. I promised them their secret was safe with me. After all, it happens to me all the time."

This time I did laugh. I couldn't help it. That was the last thing I'd expected Mac to say. "You get kissed all the time?"

36

Mac nodded. "Hazards of the job. A lot of times I'm called on to rescue damsels in distress. And they just seem to attach themselves to me. On more than one occasion I've had to break a few hearts. I can't get tied down right now, you see? My job just won't allow it. But it doesn't stop me from indulging a time or two in what those women offer me." He gave me a wink. "I just thought I should warn you. If we work together while you're here, you might end up falling for me. My good looks and charming personality make me irresistible to women."

"Thank you for warning me," I deadpanned. "I'll try and refrain from throwing myself at you."

Mac shrugged his reed-thin shoulders. "You probably won't be able to contain yourself."

I laughed again. "Just one more question, Mac. How has Dr. Stark taken the news of Nurse Noland's death?"

Mac paused before answering. "I don't know. He's been upset about a lot of things around here lately."

I picked up my pen and jotted down Dr. Stark's name. I also made a note to jot down his motive for killing Nurse Noland...when I figured it out.

"There're a lot of resourceful uses for gum."

I looked up from my notes. Mac stared at the pack of Big Red gum on my desk like a man who hadn't eaten in days.

"Would you like a piece?" I asked.

Mac thought about it for a minute. "I'll trade you four matches for two pieces of gum. I only have one match on me right now and I need it, so I'll have to give them to you later."

I shrugged. "Sure."

I had no idea why I'd need matches *or* gum. I slid two pieces of gum out and handed them to Mac.

"I better go," Mac said. "We all eat around five in the rec room. We used to eat in the cafeteria, but there aren't any windows in there and it gets a little claustrophobic. The cooks use the kitchen, but that's it. We now eat in the rec room. Want me to come by and show you where it's at?"

"Sure," I said. "But I thought Nurse Lohman said we were supposed to eat in the lounge, not the rec room? Or is that the same thing?"

Mac jumped up from my cot and gave me a thoughtful stare. "Do you *really* know a lot about curses and haunted places like you told Nurse Lohman and Billy?"

My mouth dropped. "How do you know about that?"

Mac chuckled. "I have eyes and ears everywhere."

"Clearly." I smiled and nodded my head. "Let's just say I might know a thing or two."

"Good," Mac said solemnly. "We may need you."

Before I could ask Mac any more questions, he turned and hurried out of my room.

38

CHAPTER 5

I spent the next hour sitting at the desk, jotting down what I knew so far about the murders. I knew two people had died recently, and that even though some claimed the deaths were easily explained—one an accident and the other natural causes—not everyone was convinced.

I knew Nurse Noland was hated by aide Stew Rodgers because she'd threatened to fire him if he had one more infraction. I also knew her best friend, Nurse Shue, took over her position when she died...and that Nurse Shue seemed to be stressed more than normal. Which, I suppose, was understandable. I also knew Dr. Stark and Nurse Noland were having an affair. Whether or not anyone knew outside of Mac, I wasn't sure.

I set the pen down on the desk. Not a lot to go on. Out of habit, I flicked my hand back and forth over the top of the pen, causing it to roll slightly.

That's cool. Lexi, right? See. See. I remembered.

I stopped rolling the pen and smiled as Rex jumped out of the drop-down ceiling. He landed with a soft thud on the desk.

"Hey, Rex," I said. "Find out anything?"

Not a lot. Not a lot. Nurses are scared of curses. He squeaked and chirped in a high-pitched voice, causing his mouth to gape open and his front two teeth to protrude. Seeing a rat laugh was a little disturbing.

I filled him in on what I knew so far and the list of suspects I'd made.

I'll spy on Stew and Nurse Shue.

"Listen," I said. "I'm going to need—"

"Who're you talking to?"

Rex squeaked, and I jumped up from the desk to see Mac in the doorway. Rex hopped inside my uniform pocket and burrowed down deep.

"No one. Myself."

Mac nodded and walked in the room. "I do that a lot, too. Helps me think."

"Is it five already?" I asked.

I hated not having a clock handy. Usually I just checked my cell phone if I needed the time.

"Sure is," Mac said. "We better hurry. I don't want to miss the dessert tonight. It's tapioca pudding. My favorite. Tomorrow will be chocolate pudding, and then we go back to tapioca."

"They sure know how to mix it up here, don't they?" I joked.

Mac laughed. "We'll sit with my friend Henry, if that's okay?"

"Sure. Is he a maintenance guy or an aide?"

Mac laughed. "Neither."

I jammed the gum, audio cassette, quarter, and miniature can of hairspray in my two front pockets. I didn't know exactly when I'd need the tools, so I wanted to be prepared. We walked down the hallway and passed the set of stairs that led downstairs to the front entrance and nurses station.

"Shouldn't we go down this way?" I asked.

40

Mac shook his head. "I want to avoid Nurse Shue. Last time I saw her, she was mumbling to herself behind the counter."

"Stress can do funny things to people," I said. "You did say she lost her best friend *and* she's got this new job."

Mac shrugged. "I suppose."

We walked farther down the cold, stone hallway. Just like on my side of the corridor, there was only one bulb to light the whole area. As we walked underneath, it flickered and popped.

"The second floor is practically falling down around itself," I said. "Aren't you worried?"

"Nope." Mac stopped in front of an open door. He popped his head in and out real quick. "I can get out of any situation."

He continued to walk down the hall, and I peeked into the room he'd just looked in. The kitchen and living room combo. It was empty.

We finally stopped at the end of the hallway. It was a dead end. For the first time, I had to wonder if my intuition was off. Could Mac be planning something? Was he the killer?

"Before we head down," Mac said, "can I have your word, Lexi, you won't tell anyone about this?"

"About what?" I asked, suddenly nervous what he might say or do. I liked him. I didn't want to have to take him down.

"Your word," Mac pressed.

"I promise not to tell anyone."

Mac walked near the corner of the hallway and pressed against the wall. The stones shifted smoothly, and I stared in amazement at a wide gap with a curved, stone staircase going down to the next floor.

"A hidden passage?" I whispered. "Nice. You really *have* been here a long time to have found this."

I entered the hidden passageway and waited until Mac closed the door. We were instantly encased in darkness.

"Not to worry," Mac said. "I have matches."

A few seconds later I heard a flick as the match struck a rough surface. The spark from the flame illuminated the dark passageway, and the unmistakable smell of sulfur filled the air.

I glanced down at his hand and was shocked to see a book of matches. I wasn't sure the last time I'd actually seen a book of matches.

"I steal them from Stew when he's not looking," Mac explained.

We quickly followed the curve of the staircase and reached the bottom as the match burned down and finally went out.

"Let me make sure no one is coming," Mac whispered.

I didn't hear anything, but a second later a narrow strip of light shot into the darkened passageway. There was just enough light for me to take in my surroundings. The tunnel actually curved again, and the stairs continued down to the basement. I also saw two burned matches that Mac must have dropped and forgot to pick up.

"It's clear," Mac said. "Before I forget, I already took out four matches for you."

He handed me the tiny matches then turned back toward the thin reed of light. I obviously couldn't tell him that I wouldn't need matches if I was stuck in the tunnel alone. I could just conjure up a globe of light to illuminate my way.

"Come out and slide immediately to your right against the wall, and no one should be the wiser."

I shoved the matches down inside my uniform pocket, my knuckles hitting the cassette I'd grabbed off the desk before leaving my room. I then scurried out of the tunnel and slid against the wall like he'd said. Mac swiftly turned and closed the hidden door.

I scanned the room.

It was a solarium...a huge courtyard, with windows that were tall and skinny and offered a panoramic view to the outside. The floor was made of tan and gray cobblestones. Greenery in the shape of trees and plants littered the large room. Four wrought-iron tables and chairs were assembled in the center and ornate wooden benches sat in front of each window.

I leaned away from the wall until I could see down the long hallway to my right. Sure enough, I recognized the counter to the nurses station. So this room must be what was down the hallway to my left when I first entered the nursing home with Billy. That meant the rooms where the residents stayed was down the hallway to the right of the nurses station.

"Straight through that door across from us is the rec room. It has an attached room on the right side where the cooks make the meals."

"This room is absolutely beautiful."

"Sure is," Mac agreed. "Dr. Stark really put a lot of work into this place. Hey, the cooks have the stereo on. Maybe we can do some dancing tonight. I can still Jitterbug."

"You can what?"

"The youth of today," Mac sighed.

If only you knew, Mac.

I followed him through an open archway into the rec room. Four brown and orange striped sofas were pushed against the sea-foam green walls, three gray recliners were propped in front of a large boxed television, with another tiny television on top of it. Three round tables with four plastic chairs at each sat in the middle of the room. About twenty elderly men and women sat in the available seats waiting for dinner. Cooks in the same uniform I had on pushed wheeled carts ladened down with trays of food.

I watched in horror as one elderly man dropped his roll on the couch, picked it up, and then shoved it in his mouth.

Note to self, don't sit on any of the furniture. Febreze hasn't been invented yet.

There was a narrow door to the left of the room, and I could make out three washing machines inside. I assumed the dryers were lined up along the other wall.

"There's Henry," Mac said. "Let's go sit over there."

I had a funny feeling in the pit of my stomach. Like something wasn't quite right. "These are the residents. We can't eat with them."

"Of course we can," Mac insisted. "I do it every night."

Ignoring the quizzical looks from the cooks, I sat down at a round table next to Mac and another elderly gentleman

44

with bushy salt and pepper eyebrows, wispy white hair, a white mustache, and bright blue eyes.

He grinned at me, and I couldn't hold back my gasp. He'd totally caught me unprepared. Henry had no teeth.

"Put your damn teeth in, Henry," Mac chided. "You'll give the girl a fright."

"Oopths." Henry dug his dentures out of his gray cardigan then popped them in his mouth. He gave his lips a couple smacks then stuck out his hand...the same hand he'd just used to pull out his teeth and shove in his face. "I forget sometimes. Name's Henry. Who might you be?"

"Lexi Howe."

I shook his hand, bemoaning the fact Bath & Body Works' travel-sized antibacterial hand sanitizers in titillating scents hadn't been marketed yet. I wasn't usually such a germaphobe, but I also wasn't used to being around so many people. I barely saw twenty people a week at the little museum where I worked.

I grabbed a tray from one of the cooks.

"What are you doing?" the cook hissed.

"Eating. This is my first night. I don't start until six."

The cook passed a tray to Henry and Mac, still giving me a puzzled look.

Ignoring her, I took a drink of my water and looked out the window in front of me. "Your view during your dining experience is the graveyard? Nice."

Mac laughed. "You like that, huh?"

"Doesn't get any worse than that," I said.

"Wait until you see the dungeon," Mac said. "Well, the workers call it the basement, but once you've been down there, you know it's a dungeon. Down where they used to keep the real bad ones when this place was an insane asylum."

Oh, great. Can't wait.

Me, either, Lexi! Me, either! I'll go down soon! They don't call me Rex the Explorer for nothing!

Obviously the rat didn't understand the concept of sarcasm.

Chapter 6

Henry slopped a huge dollop of mashed potatoes onto his roll. "What's a pretty little thing like you doing here?" He shoved the whole roll into his mouth and chewed.

"This is the girl that knows about curses and haunted places," Mac bragged.

"Ya don't say?" Henry leaned over and gave me a piercing look. "You gonna lift the curse off this place?"

I swirled the thick glob of mashed potatoes around on my plate and tried to work up the nerve to taste them. Testing a theory, I lifted my hand up off my spoon and smiled when the spoon stayed upright in the mashed potatoes.

"I'm interested in what's happened over the last week," I said. "If I can understand what's happened, maybe I can lift the curse."

Sounded good to me.

Henry got a faraway look in his eye. "Poor Pauley."

"Yep," Mac agreed. "Poor Pauley."

"Pauley was the other person that died?" I asked.

Henry nodded. "Died two days ago. Me and Pauley was pretty good friends I guess you could say. As much as we could be anyway after his stroke."

"What do you mean?" I asked.

"Pauley really couldn't talk anymore," Henry said, "after his stroke. But he was sharp. He still had that about him...don't think he didn't."

"Can I sit here?"

I looked up and smiled. A silver-haired woman with a Kelly-green cardigan over a black slip dress stood beside me. Her features were perfect. The green of the sweater matched her eyes, and even though she was probably in her early eighties, and her face was lined with wrinkles, there was no denying her beauty.

"Of course." I pulled out a chair for her.

"Thank you," she said demurely. "I always enjoy talking to the new people. Did you just start today?"

"I did. My name's Lexi."

The diminutive beauty put a delicate hand up to her chest. "Such a beautiful name for a beautiful girl. My name is Isabella."

"Isabella is our resident professional dancer," Mac boasted.

Isabella blushed, but I could tell she was pleased. "During World War II, I was a hostess with the USO. I was in charge of not only making sure the boys got donuts and coffee, but I also danced with a number of the soldiers. I was one of the older women and already had years of professional dance under my belt." She looked up at the ceiling. "I believe I was thirty-five back then." She gave me a wicked grin. "I found I loved to dance at an early age. So that's what I did. Worked almost thirty years in the business. I was a chorus girl for the first six or seven years right after I graduated. Worked with some amazing women. Then in nineteen fifty-one I got my big break. The Moulin Rouge reopened, and I got to perform the cancan." She closed her eyes and relished in her memories before turned back to me. "Then later on

48

when I couldn't keep up, I started teaching girls. Of course, I don't get to boogie as much as I'd like living here."

"But boy can she boogie when she does," Mac gushed.

"We were just telling Lexi about Pauley," Henry said.

Isabella touched my hand. "He used to be a cop."

"Pauley was the man," Henry boasted. "Like I said, after his stroke six months ago, it was like his mouth and brain didn't work together. He also couldn't grasp items with his right hand after that. It was a huge loss to him. The reason he had to retire from the force years ago was because he'd been shot in the line of duty. Took a bullet to his left shoulder and left hand. He never told us exactly what happened, but it was bad enough he couldn't continue his job. No matter how much physical therapy he had on his shoulder and hand, he never gained control of it again." Henry chuckled and shook his head. "But even still, he could do the coolest tricks."

"They weren't tricks," Isabella said. "They were what made him a great cop in his day."

"Like what?" I asked.

"Like before his stroke when he could still talk, there could be fifteen people in this room," Mac said, "and Pauley could walk in for two seconds and then turn around and go into the courtyard. And if one of us hid behind the kitchen door, Pauley could walk in and immediately tell who was gone! He wouldn't even have to think about it."

"That does sound neat." It also sounded like someone with a great memory and attention to detail.

Mac laughed. "But he still had it even after his stroke. This one time, Pauley was sittin' with me and Henry at the table. Someone called out his name, and when he turned to see who wanted him, me and Henry changed plates. And when Pauley turned back around to face us, he looked at our plates and laughed and laughed."

"How exactly did he die?" I asked.

"The graveyard nurse, Nurse Wilson, said he had another stroke." Mac rolled his eyes and made a face. "And then the stroke made him fall out of his chair, and he hit his head."

"But you don't think that's what happened?" I asked.

"No," Mac and Henry said at the same time.

"What do you think happened?" I asked.

"He was either scared to death, or he was pushed out of his chair," Henry said.

"Who would do something like that?" I asked.

I was beginning to think that maybe Pauley *did* die of natural causes. Having another stroke six months after the first didn't seem improbable. And then to fall out of a chair while having a stroke seemed plausible, too.

"The ghost," Henry insisted. "The same one that pushed Nurse Noland down the stairs."

Isabella and Mac both scoffed at that idea.

"A ghost didn't kill Pauley," Isabella insisted. "That's ridiculous."

I had to agree. I didn't know of a single ghost who could become corporeal enough to physically push a human being down a flight of steps or out of a chair. That took a lot of effort for a living person to do...much less someone who typically didn't have a body, per se.

"I don't even know if the police are really aware of Pauley," Mac said. "It was just a fluke they even found out he died. That Detective Hackett was back here again asking questions to Dr. Stark about Nurse Noland the morning Pauley had died."

"So you told the detective you thought Pauley's death was suspicious?"

Mac nodded. "Yes. After he asked his questions, I caught up with him and took him aside and told him there was no way Pauley just up and died. He was nice enough to listen, but that's about it. An old person dying in a nursing home isn't really cause for concern. He stopped by again today, and I tried to talk with him, but Nurse Lohman told me not to bother him. He probably doesn't even remember about Pauley."

"He does," I said. "When I spoke with him outside, he mentioned both the death of Nurse Noland and Pauley to me."

Mac's eyes widened. "Really?"

I nodded. "Really. Who found Pauley?"

"One of the aides, Judy, from the graveyard shift found him around two in the morning," Henry said. "They usually do two checkups during the middle of the night. Nurse Wilson then called an ambulance for Pauley."

I picked up my fork and cut into the leathery, gravy smothered meat. It looked even less appetizing than the mashed potatoes.

"So why all the talk about curses?" I asked.

The three of them exchanged glances.

Mac leaned in closer to me. "It's Pauley. Pauley put a curse on us all. I mean, there've always been rumors this place was haunted back when it was an asylum...but for some reason, right before he died, Pauley cursed us all."

I could tell they honestly believed what they were telling me. "Explain."

Henry took a sip of his water, his hand visibly shaking. "Like we said, Pauley couldn't really talk anymore, and when he did talk, you couldn't always understand what he was saying. His speech was slurred, and it was like his tongue couldn't move right. But we definitely understood what he was saying on the day he died. Every time he walked into a room, he'd yell out, 'curse you!' over and over."

"Just like that," Mac agreed. "He wouldn't even joke with me anymore. Just yell and curse me."

"That's something I don't understand," I said. "Nurse Lohman mentioned that nearly all the residents here are not your typical nursing home candidates. They're pretty self-sufficient. When I look around I see that's true. But from what you tell me about Pauley, he didn't fit that bill. He needed physical therapy, he'd had a stroke, he couldn't speak. Why was he here?"

Mac shrugged. "I'm not exactly sure. He'd been here since the place first opened. Pauley was pretty tight-lipped about things. I got the feeling, though, that Dr. Stark had something to do with the reason why he was here."

"What's going on here?" a shrill, female voice demanded.

I looked up and realized the voice was speaking to me.

A nurse, dressed in the same official uniform Nurse Lohman had worn that morning, stared down at me with hard eyes. This woman was younger than Nurse Lohman. Early thirties, big red hair that reached her shoulders, and I could tell she was physically fit even with the non-descript uniform on.

I put my spoon down and slowly stood up. "I was just having dinner. I'm new here, and the lady who hired me, Nurse Lohman, said I didn't have to clock in until six."

"I'm aware," the woman said. "I'm the head nurse in charge of the night crew, Sandy Shue."

The I-may-have-killed-my-best-friend, Nurse Sandy Shue? Why am I not surprised?

"And who gave you permission to eat with the residents?" Nurse Shue asked.

I looked over at Mac...who just happened to be too busy staring at his tapioca to help me out. Henry and Isabella also suddenly looked too busy to make eye contact. I'd known Henry and Isabella were residents, but I couldn't figure out Mac. After all, he had on a uniform, and he was up on the second floor. Of course, he'd also showed me a hidden tunnel.

"I'm sorry," I said, feeling the sudden need to protect these people. "I wasn't aware it wasn't allowed."

A sudden commotion by the door cut off what Nurse Shue was about to say.

"Where is he?" a man demanded.

Before anyone could say anything, the guy spotted Mac and charged after him. I caught the guy's scent before he reached me. He had on enough cologne to choke a chicken.

Mac quickly stood up, shrugged out of the enormous white jacket, and handed it to the angry man.

"Why, I ought to—"

"That's enough, Stew," Nurse Shue said.

"I don't know how you do it," Stew said to Mac, "but one day I'm gonna catch you. And when I do, you'll—"

"I said that was enough," Nurse Shue said sharply.

Put up your dukes! Put up your dukes! They don't call me Rex the Killer Rat for nothing!

I put my hand over my pocket to keep Rex inside. The last thing I needed was a lunatic rat scurrying about beating up on Stew.

Stew scowled at Nurse Shue but didn't argue further. Instead, he shoved his muscular arms through the jacket and pulled it taut over his body. His lip curled into a sneer, which caused his black mustache to wiggle like a bushy caterpillar across his face.

Without another word, Stew turned around. I couldn't help myself. I mentally knocked Henry's cane to the ground and had it roll in front of Stew. He couldn't react in time, and I bit back a smile as we all watched in horrific glee as he sputtered and flailed his arms in the air...before finally falling face-first onto the ground. He laid sprawled on the floor for a good three seconds. Enough time for me to catch sight of a long string of hair hanging down the back of his neck. Almost like his neck had a tail.

Stew quickly stood up, brushed himself off, and looked around to see who'd pushed the cane in front of him. No one said a word. He finally smoothed down his hair, whipped back around—causing his tail to fly out from his head—and stalked out the door.

Nurse Shue continued to glare at me. "I was told you were in your room on the second floor. How did you get down the stairs and past the nurses station without me seeing?"

I looked at Mac. He gave me a sheepish look I couldn't help but love. No way would I rat on him that he'd obviously sneaked up to the second floor and didn't have a room up there like I thought.

I shrugged. "I don't know. When I came down the stairs no one was at the nurses station. I wasn't sure which way to go, so I started wandering around. Mac here invited me to dinner."

Nurse Shue snorted. "Mac? He told you his name and you still went with him? Didn't think anything odd about that?"

I frowned. "Odd about the name Mac? No."

Nurse Shue narrowed her eyes. "You are aware he tells people his name is Angus MacGyver?"

"Yes."

"Are you telling me you don't know who Angus MacGyver is?" Nurse Shue asked.

"A maintenance man?" I guessed. "At least that's what I thought he did here. He said he can fix just about anything as long as he has his duct tape."

Nurse Shue let out a disgusted breath, grabbed me by my arm, and dragged me over to the teeny tiny television. "*MacGyver* is a television show. That man over there telling you his name is Mac is delusional. He's not a fix-it man. He doesn't work here. He *lives* here as a resident."

Note to self, brush up on 80s television when you get back home so this doesn't happen again.

CHAPTER 7

I cut my eyes back to Mac. He was still busy shoveling food into his mouth. While a part of me was embarrassed for being duped by him, I didn't particularly like the way she made Mac sound. Like he was just a crazy old man.

"He seemed perfectly sensible to me," I said. "Now, do I have a list of duties to follow tonight? Something that tells me what to do?"

Besides hunt down clues and find a killer.

My pocket rustled.

Me, too! Me, too! I got your back, kid. Yes, I do. They don't call me Rex the Defender for nothing.

I rested my hand on the outside of my pocket and lovingly cupped Rex in my palm. He may have taken some getting used to, but he was a good protector.

"What did Nurse Lohman tell you about the facility?" Nurse Shue asked.

I shrugged. "Not a lot."

"Then let me give you the rundown of how it works here. We're a small, privately-owned nursing home. In fact, Dr. Stark doesn't even like to call it a nursing home."

"Okay."

"We are still in the experimental stages of running a facility like this, but basically this is a place where the older generation has a chance to live without being in an actual nursing home. Dr. Stark is on staff ten to eleven hours a day. He's here from eight to noon, and then he ends his day back here from three until ten or later. He bought this facility in nineteen eighty-five and totally renovated it. He's not only the doctor on staff, but he's also the administrator. He oversees the business side of the facility as well as the medical side. He's a very busy man."

"So Dr. Stark is the owner?" I asked.

"Yes, he is. We have registered nurses like myself on duty twenty-four hours a day, seven days a week. One on morning duty, two on evening shift..." Nurse Shue's voice trailed off. "At least, we used to have two on evening shift. Unfortunately, with the death of Nurse Noland, we now only have me. There's also a registered nurse on graveyard. Since this type of facility is still in the experimental stages, we are extremely small. We only run about twenty beds."

"It all sounds great," I said.

It also sounded like a modern-day assisted living facility. The concept must have been so new in the late eighties no one knew what to call it.

Nurse Shue spent the next fifteen minutes outlining my night-shift duties. After the residents finished eating, I was to help them back to their rooms and assist them in whatever capacity they needed. It was the same at bedtime. I also needed to gather all linens and clothes and put them in the large laundry bins sitting in the hallways.

It seemed straightforward enough, with enough gaps in the evening to give me time to snoop around. Delusional or not, Mac was obviously the guy to keep in mind when maneuvering covertly through the massive nursing home.

After Nurse Shue left me alone, I marched over to Mac's table. The guilty party was still busy devouring his tapioca pudding.

"Want some?" Mac asked as he thrust his bowl at me.

58

I wanted to be mad at him, but I just didn't have it in me. "No, thanks. I need to help people back to their rooms."

"Don't worry," Henry said, "most will go willingly."

I furrowed my brow. "What do you mean *most*?"

He gave me a toothy grin but didn't say anything else.

"Hi," a perky voice said behind me. "Are you, like, totally new here?"

An overly hairsprayed and permed blonde with bangs up to the sky, heavy blue eyeliner, and bubble-gum pink eyeshadow with matching pink lip gloss bounced in front of me. She was by far the youngest person I'd seen working at the nursing home.

"I am," I said.

"Like, that's so cool! My name's Nikki!" I swear the girl could end every sentence in an exclamation point. She seemed so dang chipper and happy.

"Lexi. Lexi Howe."

I held out my hand for her to shake. She looked confused for half a second, then grabbed it and shook it up and down a little too enthusiastically.

"Lexi? Like, that's a totally cool name. I've never heard that name before."

"So I keep hearing," I said dryly. "You're a little young to be working here, aren't you?"

"Nope," Nikki said. "Been here, like, about a year now. Usually I just work a couple hours in the evenings when I'm in school. But since it's summer, like, I can totally work more."

"You're still in high school?" I asked.

"Yep." When I didn't say anything, she reached out and caught me in the ribs. "Psych! You silly! Of *course* I'm not, like, still in high school!" I marveled at the way her hair hardly moved as her head bounced side to side when she talked. "I just graduated. Like, I'll be starting college next month."

This girl seriously needed to lay off the caffeine. And if she used the word 'like' one more time between breaths, I was going to nut out. Big time.

"Well, I should get back to work," I said as politely as I could. The girl was giving me a huge headache. If I had to be around her anymore, I was either going to start ripping out my own mile-high hairdo or worse—start talking like her.

"Me, too," Nikki squeaked. "Maybe we can talk later about movies? I *love* going to the show, don't you? It can get a little expensive, though. It's now, like, *four dollars* to see a movie. Can you imagine?"

Just wait, sweetheart. Soon you'll need to take out a bank loan to get popcorn.

"Watch out for the runners," Nikki said as she gave me a perky wave.

"Runners?" I asked. But she was already gone.

I turned back to the table. "Is she always like that?"

Isabella laughed softly. "Yes. Oh, to be young and beautiful again."

"You're young and beautiful to me," Mac said.

Isabella blushed and continued to slowly eat her tapioca.

"I better go see after some of these people." I turned to Mac. "But you and I will talk later. Understand?"

60

Mac grinned and continued shoving in his tapioca.

I sauntered over to an extremely thin man sitting on one of the couches. His food tray was gone, and he wasn't watching television. I figured he was ready to go back to his room.

"Can I help you back to your room?" I asked.

"What?" He held up his hand to his ear.

I leaned in closer and upped my voice. "Can I help you to your room?"

He shook his head. "Still can't hear ya, girlie."

I sighed and yelled at the top of my lungs. "Can I help you to your room!"

Everyone stopped moving, and the room grew eerily quiet. You could've heard a church mouse run through the room.

"Why're you yelling at me?" the man demanded. "I heard you the first time."

Suddenly the room erupted in laughter. It took me a second to realize the man had been teasing me. He'd heard me just fine the first time.

I forced a smile. "Ha ha. Good one."

Stars above...this is gonna be a long assignment.

"Maybe Ernie here wants to go back to his room," Jokester said, pointing to a near-comatose black man sitting next to him.

"Sir," I asked tentatively, "do you need help back to your room?"

The man's eyes snapped open, and before I could grasp what his intentions were, he took off like a bullet. Again, everyone laughed around me.

Runner! Runner! We got us a runner! Rex jumped out of my dress pocket and scurried after the man. *I'll take him down! Rex to the rescuuuuuuuue!*

Before I could follow after Ernie or shout at Rex to stop, Jokester guy pointed to my pocket.

"Did a rat just jump out of your pocket?" Jokester asked.

"What?" I deadpanned. "I can't hear you."

The old lady on the couch next to Jokester cackled with laughter. "She got you, Norman."

Norman, aka Jokester, looked sheepishly at me. "You'll fit in just fine here."

Thirty minutes later everyone was back in their rooms, and I was ready for a break. I hadn't been this exhausted in a long time. Not only was this job physically demanding, but it was emotionally exhausting, too. I'd had three runners—one of them a streaker. An image I won't get out of my head for a long time.

Rex had returned from chasing down Ernie, and was curled up in my front pocket napping.

"Wanna take a ten minute break with me?" Nikki asked as she sidled up to me in the women's hallway.

Whaddya know, she can speak a sentence without the word like in it.

"Sure," I said.

The residents all lived on the west side of the building. Down the main hallway from the nurses station there were twelve rooms, six on each side where the women slept. A narrow passage jutting left, halfway down the women's hallway, was the men's section. There were twelve more rooms down that hallway.

We'd just passed the nurses station when I felt the hairs on the back of my neck stand on end. I closed my eyes and concentrated.

"What's wrong?" Nikki asked.

"Shh," I said.

Sauntering over to the chest-high counter, I stood on my tiptoes to peer over. "Is that you, Mac?"

Mac popped up from the ground. "How'd you know I was down here?"

"I heard you rustling around," I lied.

"This is where Nurse Shue keeps my duct tape and Swiss Army knife."

"Like, we're so gonna get in trouble if we get caught," Nikki whined.

"Go on," I said. "I'll meet you in the solarium in a second."

Nikki didn't need any further prompting. She turned and practically ran down the hallway into the solarium.

I closed my eyes and concentrated, trying to see if I could sense where Nurse Shue was. I had nothing.

"Got it!" Mac cried.

"Hurry," I hissed. "I don't know how much longer you have."

I heard Mac grunt and curse.

"What's wrong?" I asked, my own voice rising in panic.

"The drawer's stuck!"

I was about to help him out with a little wave of my hand, when I felt prickles on the back of my neck again. I closed my eyes.

Nurse Shue and another person were ascending the stairs from the basement!

"Hurry!" I cried as I whipped my hand through the air, causing the drawer to suddenly fly open. "Nurse Shue will be here in five seconds!"

Mac gathered up his duct tape and knife and tossed them over the counter to me. "Keep them safe. And distract her for me."

"How?"

CHAPTER 8

I shoved the duct tape in one pocket and the knife in the other just as Nurse Shue and a man dressed in a long white coat hit the top of the steps.

Watch it! Rat trying to sleep here. Hey! A running wheel. Cool! They don't call me Rex the Runner for nothing!

Nurse Shue and the man both turned and caught me leaning casually against the counter of the nurses station. At least I hoped I looked casual.

"Miss Howe," Nurse Shue said. "What're you doing?"

I tried to ignore the movement in my pocket as Rex scurried to get inside the duct tape.

It's broken! Broken. Broken. Broken. Broken.

"Nothing." I rested my hands nonchalantly over my pockets so they couldn't see all the movement inside. "Just thought I'd see if I could do anything for you."

Nurse Shue looked around, as though expecting at any moment to catch someone doing something nefarious.

"Well, isn't that thoughtful," the handsome man beside her said.

Nurse Shue sighed and put her hand on Dr. Stark's arm. "This is a new hire, Lexi Howe. She just started tonight. Lexi, this is Dr. Stark."

I stuck my hand out and prayed that Mac would stay huddled under the desk. "It's nice to meet you, Dr. Stark."

Dr. Stark smiled as he shook my hand.

I guessed him to be in his mid-thirties. Way too young to have opened this place up on his own after medical school. He had to have school loans out the hind end. Where on earth did he get the money to buy this place, fix it up, and run it?

"So nice to have you with us." He had thick, dark hair, brown eyes, and a full mustache. He stood nearly six feet tall, and I could tell he was physically fit even with the lab coat on. Plus, he had the cutest dimples when he smiled.

I could actually place this 80s look-alike. He reminded me of Tom Selleck. No wonder Nurse Noland had been gaga over him.

I made a pretense of looking around them toward the steps that led downstairs. "What's down in the basement?"

Nurse Shue drew in a sharp breath. "Nothing for you to worry about. You will not need to go down there."

Dr. Stark chuckled. "It's okay, Nurse Shue. I keep my office down there. It's nice and quiet, and I can look over the charts in peace. Or if there are any administrative duties I need to oversee as the owner of the facility, I can do so without interruption. Plus, the infirmary is down there. If a resident needs a little extra care, there's a room for them downstairs."

I scrunched up my nose. "I get a vibe it's pretty spooky down there."

"It does take some getting used to," Dr. Stark agreed. "The west wing is completely closed off. I haven't been able to renovate that area yet." Dr. Stark chuckled. "I hear you had your first run-in with Mac."

I bit my lip. I didn't want to sound like I was talking about Mac behind his back, especially since he was huddled only three feet from where I stood. "Yes. He got me good. But I really like him. Seems like a sweet man."

66

"I don't have anything for you right now," Nurse Shue said sharply as she moved to stand behind the nurses station. "You may take your break."

Nurse Shue was almost to the back of the counter. A few more steps and she'd be able to see Mac.

I need a distraction!

Distraction, Lexi? Distraction you say? Distraction is my middle name!

Before I could blink, Rex hopped out of my pocket and scurried across the floor to stand in front of Nurse Shue.

"Is that a rat?" Dr. Stark asked.

I thought for sure Nurse Shue would scream at the sight of Rex. Instead, she pivoted from the back of the counter and headed toward a large, metal cabinet.

"I have a trap in here somewhere," Nurse Shue said. "I'll have that thing killed in minutes."

I was about to protest, when Rex stood up on his hind legs, raised his tiny fisted paw in the air, shook it profusely, and emitted squeaks of outrage.

Ha! Better women have tried to capture me and failed! Do your best devil woman!

A snort of laughter flew out of my mouth before I could stop it. When Dr. Stark looked at me, I tried covering up the snort by coughing into my hand.

Nurse Shue whirled around, rat trap in hand, and took off after Rex. Rex gave another squeal, turned, and fled down the hall toward the west wing.

I'll never give up! Never surrender! Rex the Rat forever!

I had to bite the inside of my cheek and count to five so I wouldn't burst out laughing. Rex the Rat was one funny guy.

"Well," Dr. Stark said, "that should keep Nurse Shue busy for a while."

I nodded. "I guess I better get going. I told Nikki I'd take my break with her if Nurse Shue didn't need me for anything."

"Very well."

I knew I should encourage him to leave and let Mac get up from under the counter, but I wanted to feel Dr. Stark out a little more.

"I'm sorry to hear about Nurse Noland," I said.

Dr. Stark winced. "Yes, her death was a great loss to this facility."

That's heartfelt...not.

"I heard you two were pretty close," I hedged. "Her death must have hit you hard."

Dr. Stark's jaw twitched and his eyes went flat. "Nurse Noland and I were colleagues. Nothing more."

"Of course," I said.

But I knew that wasn't true. Or was it? Should I really trust a guy who thinks he's a television star who can stop a bomb with a paperclip?

It might be time to rethink this.

"Well, you don't have to worry about me. I don't believe in curses or haunted places," I said. "I hear the patient who died recently, Pauley, went around cursing people the day he died."

68

Something flashed in Dr. Stark's eye. If I didn't know better I'd say it was regret. But regret for what? Killing Pauley or not being able to save him?

"I need to check on a few more residents before I leave," Dr. Stark said dismissively. "Good to have you on board at Gravestone Manor."

Without another word, Dr. Stark spun on his heel and hurried down the hallway, his dress shoes echoing loudly off the cold, hard surface.

"That was close," Mac said as he hopped up.

I motioned for him to hurry from behind the counter.

"Are you *sure* about Nurse Noland and Dr. Stark?" I asked once Mac stood in front of me again.

"Positive. Saw it with my own eyes."

I frowned. "Then Dr. Stark must be lying. Or at least he doesn't want us to know about him and Nurse Noland. I wonder why?"

"I probably shouldn't have even told you. I haven't told anyone else, not even Detective Hackett." Mac held out his hand. "Can I have my duct tape and knife back?"

"Oh, right." I dug in my pocket and retrieved the items. "Be careful."

Mac cocked his head to the side. "Something tells me I should be saying that to you."

I sighed. "True. Listen, Dr. Stark wasn't happy when I pressed him about Nurse Noland. He may put two and two together and figure out it was you who told me. He knew we'd already been together today."

"That's true." Mac frowned.

"Mac, who found Nurse Noland's body?"

"Nurse Wilson. She went to the dungeon sometime during the middle of the night."

"And Pauley's body was found by an aide named Judy?" I asked.

"Yep," Mac said. "Judy worked the graveyard shift. She really believes the place was haunted and cursed. That's why she quit."

I needed to speak to this Judy woman. It seemed to me that the two deaths had occurred during the graveyard shift. While I believed my suspects so far with motives of some kind were Dr. Stark, Nurse Shue, and Stew Rodgers, I also needed to rule out Nurse Wilson and this Judy person.

"You think there's something more than just a curse going on here, don't you?" Mac asked.

I shrugged. "I don't know. I just find it odd two people died within a couple days of each other, and many are quick to blame it on a curse or haunting and not look further."

Hope flickered in Mac's eyes. "You think there's a connection between the two deaths?"

I hesitated. Mainly because I was afraid Mac would want to help me out. "I honestly don't know. But I *do* wonder what the police really think about Nurse Noland's death."

Mac shrugged, but I could tell he was taking this seriously. "From what I overheard the detective say when he questioned Nurse Lohman and Dr. Stark, the police think Nurse Noland accidentally fell down the stairs. I also overheard Nurse Shue tell the detective that Nurse Noland wasn't feeling well the night she died, and when they retired up to their rooms, Nurse Noland told Nurse Shue she was going to sneak down to the infirmary and get some medicine.

70

So it sounds like Nurse Noland tiptoed to the basement and then accidentally tripped going down the stairs."

"Easy enough for the police to believe," I said.

Mac shrugged again. "As far as Pauley's death goes, I told the detective when I spoke to him, that Stew was the last one to see Pauley alive."

"Whoa! Really?"

"He told Nurse Shue that Pauley refused help to get ready for bed and insisted on sitting in his chair. When Stew checked on him again around ten or eleven and tried to coax Pauley to bed, again Pauley became belligerent and started yelling at Stew like he did us. Stew left. Then Pauley supposedly had a stroke and died."

"When said aloud, it doesn't really seem like there's a connection," I said.

"But I also knew Pauley. Considered him a friend. There had to be a reason why he was so upset and angry the last day of his life."

I nodded. "I can see why you'd want to believe that."

"If you're gonna look for a possible killer, I'd like to help. It's what I do, ya know? I'm good in these kinds of situations."

And there it was...the offer I didn't want to accept. I already had a spastic rat running around wreaking havoc. The last thing I needed was a wanna-be Indiana Jones as a sidekick.

I knew about Indiana Jones thanks to an ex-boyfriend. About the only good thing in that ten-minute relationship was the introduction of Harrison Ford to my life.

I reluctantly nodded. I just couldn't say no. "Okay. If I think I've stumbled upon something, I'll let you know."

"Same with me," Mac said. "If I find a clue or overhear anything important, I'll be sure and tell you."

We shook on it.

"I better go," Mac said, "before Nurse Shue notices I'm not in my room. Thanks for distracting them for me."

"Don't do anything rash," I said.

Mac gave me a salute and scurried down the hallway. I hurried into the solarium to take my break with Nikki.

"There you are," Nikki said. "Like, I thought you got lost or something."

"Nope." I pulled out a chair and winced when the metal chair slid across the stone. "I ran into Nurse Shue and Dr. Stark."

Nikki's eyes grew wide. "Isn't Dr. Stark a stud muffin?"

I grinned at her choice of words. I had to admit, the more I was around Nikki, the more I liked her vocabulary.

"Um, yes. He seems like quite the stud muffin." I bit my cheek to keep from laughing. "But I heard he was seeing Nurse Noland."

Nikki gasped. "What? I never heard that." Nikki bit her lip and looked outside before continuing. "Although, that makes a little more sense considering the conversation I overheard the night before she died."

CHAPTER 9

"Whaddya mean?" I asked.

Nikki bit her lip again, as though trying to decide whether or not to tell me. "I don't want to sound like I'm gossiping, but, like, a day before Nurse Noland died, I overheard her and Nurse Shue talking. I honestly didn't know it was about Dr. Stark until you just said his name."

"What were they talking about?" I asked.

"Like, just hushed voices at first. Then I saw Nurse Noland start to cry, but Nurse Shue wasn't all that sympathetic. She told Nurse Noland she should have known it would happen sooner or later, and that the two couldn't be. But then they saw me and shut up."

"So possibly Nurse Noland and Dr. Stark broke up?"

"I guess," Nikki said. "I did hear something strange, though. I heard Nurse Noland say she couldn't believe he would accuse her of cheating on him, and she wondered who would tell him such a horrible lie. Again, I didn't know who 'he' was at the time."

My brows shot up. "So Dr. Stark broke up with Nurse Noland because someone told him she cheated?"

Nikki nodded. "It sounded that way."

In order for Dr. Stark to give it credence, surely the person telling him had to be a very reliable person.

"And Nurse Noland was found at the bottom of the stairs going to the basement?" I asked.

"Yes."

Now I had no choice but to sneak down to the basement soon and snoop around for clues. And though I'd never thought of myself as a sissy, I'd seen too many scary movies about torture chambers in old asylums not to be a little freaked.

"How long have you lived in River Springs?" Nikki asked.

"Just moved here," I said.

I was about to ask her about her family when Stew walked up to our table.

"Hey, Nikki," he said in a low growl as he cocked an eyebrow. "Mind if I sit down?"

"Yes, we do," I said.

Stew glared down at me. "Well, I wasn't really talkin' to you now, was I?"

Without waiting to hear Nikki's reply, Stew went to plop down in the vacant chair next to us. Disgusted, I concentrated on the chair and slid it backward.

Stew landed hard on his butt. "What the—"

I snickered as he made a show of hauling himself up off the floor. Pulling the chair behind him, he went to sit down. For a penny, I'd have moved the chair again. But I didn't want to press my luck.

Stew stuck his feet out straight in front of him and crossed them at the ankles. Folding his hands across his stomach, he gave Nikki a smirk.

"What's that stench?" I asked as I crinkled my nose.

"Polo by Ralph Lauren," Stew boasted. "It's all the rage."

"I'm pretty sure Mr. Lauren doesn't want you bathing in it," I deadpanned.

Nikki giggled.

74

Stew snarled at me before turning his attention back to Nikki. "I'm thinkin' of going to Blockbuster tomorrow night and renting that new movie *Die Hard*. My buddy works there, and he said they got like seven VHS tapes in. He said he'd set one back for me if I wanted. Maybe you wanna come upstairs after my shift, have a little Boone's Farm Strawberry wine, watch a movie?"

Omigod, it's the 80s version of Netflix and chill!

"Yeah, like, I don't think so," Nikki said. "But thanks anyway."

Stew scowled. "Why not?"

"Because she's obviously not into you," I said.

Anger flashed in Stew's eyes. I didn't need to have witchy powers to know this guy was a predator. I had no doubt he could kill if he needed to.

"It's that police guy who was here the other day, isn't it?" Stew demanded.

Nikki's face turned red, but I caught a glimpse of a smile around her lips.

Psst! It's me, Rex. Open your pocket. Need to hide. Nurse is crazy! Crazy I say!

I surreptitiously held out my front pocket for Rex. When I didn't feel him jump in, I started to panic, wondering what had suddenly happened to the little beast.

Blasphemy! What's he got on his neck? What? What?

I tilted my head and looked at the back of Stew's head. "What's that hanging down from your neck?"

Stew reached up and pulled a piece of long, stringy hair out to the side of his head. "It's my rat tail. You like?"

Imposter! You must die! Die I say!

75

Rex jumped up on the table, dashed across the tabletop, and leaped off the edge...catching the end of Stew's rat tail in his pink paws.

Yee-haw! I got ya now! Prepare to die!

Stew let out a shrill, girly scream that I was sure woke the dead in the graveyard out back. He jumped up from his chair, turning in circles like a dog chasing its tail, trying to fling Rex off his hair. Rex, bless his heart, held on for dear life...his own rat tail whipping through the air.

Gimme a knife! I'll cut it off! Cut it off, I say. They don't call me Rex the Barber for nothing!

"What's going on here?" Nurse Shue called out from the doorway of the solarium.

Stew stopped in his tracks, and Rex chose that moment to make his escape. From his precarious position at the end of Stew's rat tail, he dropped down to the ground and scurried away.

"Nothing," Stew said.

"Nikki, Lexi," Nurse Shue snapped, "go check the rec room and make sure it's empty."

"Yes, ma'am." Nikki jumped up and motioned for me to follow.

I gave Stew one more death glare before following Nikki. The only people left in the multi-purpose recreational room were the cooks in the kitchen. I walked over to the arched doorway on the right and poked my head in. Two cooks were at an industrial-sized sink spraying trays, while another cook wiped down the room.

"We're good," Nikki said.

I headed over to the window she was currently gazing out. There was a small parking lot behind the building, along with the massive graveyard. A handful of cars and trucks were parked in the parking lot.

"Can you imagine, like, driving such a nice car?" Nikki asked.

I smiled on the inside. It was always hard when people talked about how incredible something was not to immediately go, "Wait until you see what's coming up!"

"Yeah," I agreed. "That's a pretty cool Jeep."

I didn't think she was talking about the four-door station wagon, or the rusted-out lime green Pinto, or the orange Gremlin, or the dented-up pickup truck, or the other three cars in the lot that were all just as non-descript.

"That's Dr. Stark's. He said it's only two years old." She turned to me. "He's so amazing."

I heard the wistfulness in her voice. I didn't know if it was for the man or the car.

"You got a boyfriend?" I asked.

Nikki's cheeks turned pink again. "No. Not really. But I do have to say, like, the younger detective guy that came by the other day with Detective Hackett was hecka cute. And he gave me his number."

Nikki looked around before pulling a piece of paper out of her pocket. "He told me he'd just passed his test, and he was now a junior detective. He came out both times to the nursing home when, like, Nurse Noland and Pauley died. He gave me his number and said it rings *directly* to his desk phone. Can you believe it?"

I glanced down at the paper. It was a handwritten number on ruled paper with the name Detective Seaver scrawled across the top.

Nikki leaned down and picked up a pen and paper off one of the tables in the room. She scribbled something down and handed it to me. "It's my phone number. Just in case you want to get out of here sometime. Maybe grab a Frito pie down at the Frosty Freeze."

"Okay, thanks." I had no idea what a Frito pie was, but I loved all sorts of pie, so I was game. "Who else works the night shift? There's Nurse Shue, Stew, you, me. Anyone else?"

"There used to be Nurse Noland, of course. They usually keep two nurses on staff in the evenings. But, like, since Nurse Noland died, it's just Nurse Shue right now. There used to be more, but they've quit within the last three days. Oh, there's this guy, Mark, who's like a janitor. Usually he just pops in to mop the floors at night. But I think that's all right now. Since the deaths started last week, we've lost quite a few staff members."

I thought about what I knew as far as assisted living facilities went. It seemed this one was kind of boring. They had the people all doing the same thing at the same time, and there wasn't a lot of activities. I wasn't sure yet how it was different from a traditional nursing home. The assisted living facilities I knew had more freedom.

"Don't they have like a bingo night or a karaoke night or anything fun like that? Craft night?"

Nikki's eyes lit up. "Dr. Stark has been talking about trying that stuff. He said, like, the older people need to

78

exercise and interact with each other more than just television and eating. They could do that at a nursing home. He wants this place to be more like what their daily lives were once like." She shrugged. "I think he just needs help setting it all up."

"Like an activities director," I said. "I bet you could do something like that."

"That would be, like, so totally awesome!"

Nikki lifted her sleeve and checked her watch.

"Whoa!" I grabbed her arm. "That's a colorful watch."

The band was bubble-gum pink, the face plate was pale aqua, and there were tiny shapes of various colors where the numbers should have been.

"It's my newest Swatch watch," she said proudly. "Got it for graduation a couple months ago. I have three now."

I had to admit, the decade was fascinating. I wanted more than ever now to talk Mrs. Carmichael into doing an 80s display at the Clay County Historical Society.

"We should probably go gather bed sheets and clothes that need to be washed," Nikki said. "We start that every night during our shift, then let the graveyard shift finish washing and drying since it's, like, quieter during those hours."

"Have you noticed a difference in Nurse Shue's demeanor lately?" I asked as we headed toward the living quarters on the west side of the building.

Nikki didn't say anything until we passed the nurses station. Luckily no one was behind the counter.

"Not really," Nikki said. "I mean, now that Nurse Noland has died and she's in charge, there are small changes in her behavior. But that's normal, I guess."

We meandered around a large laundry cart piled high with sheets in the hallway.

"What about right before Nurse Noland's death? Did you notice a difference even back then?"

We paused outside a room. "Not really. But then again, I don't really know Nurse Shue that well. Or Nurse Noland. I usually only worked, like, a few hours in the evening after school, and those ladies didn't really socialize with me. Nurse Noland would give me my list of duties, and that was it."

"That makes sense."

"Why do you ask? Did you know Nurse Noland or something?"

"No," I said. "It was just something Mac said to me, that's all."

Nikki giggled. "I like Mac, but he's kinda a space cadet. Imagine thinking he's MacGyver in real life!"

"Yeah...imagine."

We opened one of the doors along the hallway and stepped inside. Isabella sat in a rocking chair and hummed softly to herself. She opened her eyes when she heard us enter.

"Oh, girls. So nice of you to come see me tonight. I was just thinking about my dancing days."

I glanced around the room and marveled at Isabella's collections. There at least thirty little raisins in all manner of poses, some holding instruments.

"Are those raisins?" I asked.

80

"I love the California Raisins, don't you? Isabella asked. "The way they move and dance around."

Atop her dresser and nightstand were various sized troll dolls sporting myriad colors of five-inch tufts of hair. Most were naked, but a few had on tiny colored shirts that matched their hair.

"The troll dolls are magical," Isabella said. "Plus, I love the color of their hair. I wish I could have magenta hair."

I furrowed my brow. "Why can't you?"

Nikki and Isabella gaped at me.

"You mean have her look like a punk rocker?" Nikki giggled.

Isabella grinned. "Can you imagine?"

"Psst," Mac said as he poked his head inside the door.

Nikki gasped. "Mac, don't get caught being in here. You'll, like, get in trouble. You know Nurse Shue and Stew don't like you guys being out of your rooms after eight o'clock."

Mac winked at Nikki. "I've gotten in and out of more sticky situations than you can shake a stick at."

I closed my eyes and got a sense of where everyone was. I had the impression that Nurse Shue and Stew were both down in the men's ward. I had no idea how long it would be before they realized Mac was gone.

"I just happen to have this little Walkman handy," Mac said. "Too bad we don't have a tape to listen to."

He looked pointedly at me.

"I think I have a mixed tape." I dug in my front pocket, pulled out the cassette, and handed it to Mac. "Will this work? I have no idea what's on it, but you can try it if you want."

Mac popped the tape into the bulky contraption.

"I love this song," Nikki gushed. "Don't you?"

"Yeah," I said.

I must have looked dumbfounded because Nikki gawked at me. "This is Foreigner's *I Want to Know What Love Is*. You know this song, right?"

"Of course," I said and pretended to hum along.

"Care to dance?" Mac asked Isabella.

Isabella clapped her hands in glee and rose to her feet. Mac handed the Walkman to Nikki, put one hand on Isabella's shoulder and the other on her waist, and moments later the two were shuffling around.

"Like, that's so romantic." Nikki wiped her eyes, and I couldn't help but think it was the perfect use for the tape.

The way I figured it, the quarter had been used, and now the cassette tape. I also thought maybe the gum clue had already been used, seeing as how I traded a couple matches with Mac for some gum. How that was handy, I had no idea. Now all that was left was the miniature can of Aqua Net hairspray.

The hairs on the back of my neck and arms stood up. Closing my eyes, I sensed Nurse Shue was on her way to the women's hallway.

"Guys, I hate to cut this short," I said. "But I think Nurse Shue is coming this way."

Of course, I didn't just *think* it...I *knew* it.

As if in slow motion, I glanced down at the doorknob and was shocked to see the knob starting to turn. My eyes

82

shot to Mac, and before any of us could react, he dropped down to the ground and shimmied under the bed.

"What's going on in here?" Nurse Shue asked. "I thought I heard music."

Nikki turned off the Walkman in her hand. "I just wanted to play a song for Isabella tonight."

That explanation would have been sufficient if Nikki's voice hadn't sounded five decibels too high and her face wasn't bright red.

Nurse Shue looked around the room, her hawk-like eyes taking in everything. "Lexi, Mrs. Dial next door needs help getting ready for bed. Please assist. And make sure you bring out her old bedding to be washed."

Hoping for the best, I hurried out of the room and next door to Mrs. Dial's room. I helped her turn down her bed, but I wasn't done for the night. What I'd learned during my brief stint at the assisted living facility was that most of these residents didn't really need help getting ready for bed or help to and from eating times...they were self-sufficient. What they really wanted and needed was an ear. So for the next fifteen minutes, Mrs. Dial proceeded to tell me all about the time she had a boil on her butt lanced.

Yay me.

CHAPTER 10

"Psst," Mac said, peeking his head out of Isabella's door. "Is the coast clear? Nurse Shue sent Nikki home for the night since it was almost time for her to clock out anyway. So I don't have a lookout."

I closed my eyes for a second. I couldn't sense anyone around. Making a show of looking around so Mac wouldn't think it odd I just closed my eyes and said the coast was clear, I gestured him with my hand. "Hurry."

Mac took off like a man half his age, scurrying down the men's hallway, avoiding another laundry cart sitting out. I glanced over and caught Isabella's eye. She looked happy and a bit smitten.

"Here's your tape back, dear," Isabella said. "I hope you don't mind, but Mac and I fast forwarded it and wrote down what songs were on the tape for you. That's quite an eclectic array."

I took the tape and squinted. Sure enough, all scrunched together so it looked like one big word, she'd written down each song title.

"Thanks. Night, Isabella."

Isabella waved and shut her door.

Knowing I needed to strike while the coast was clear, I jogged down the men's hallway and stopped in front of the door Mac had disappeared into seconds before.

"Mac? You in there?" I knocked softly on the door. "It's Lexi."

Mac yanked open the door, his grin infectious. "I may have to think of giving up my bachelor ways if Miss Isabella keeps after me like she is."

I snorted. "Listen, can you tell me which room was Pauley's? I want to check it out."

Mac lost his smile and turned serious. "I'll show you."

"No, I don't want you to get caught."

Plus, I could sense a presence long before Mac could see them.

Mac put his hand on my arm. "I'm coming to keep an eye on you. Don't argue. Plus, you're gonna need me to get in. The room is locked. For some reason, Dr. Stark hasn't had the room cleaned out yet. He just told the nurses to lock it and make sure no one disrupted anything."

Again, I couldn't very well admit I could probably be in the room before he even took out his knife to break in. Sighing, I gestured for him to follow me. "Then let's go before Nurse Shue or Stew comes back."

Mac grinned and shut his door behind him. I had to wonder why it was Dr. Stark had ordered the room locked and not cleared. Had he left important evidence behind that might indicate he was the killer? And if so, why wait? Why hadn't he removed what he needed and cleared the room?

We walked back toward the women's hallway but stopped before we reached the cross section. "This is—was Pauley's room."

"Okay. Do your thing and open the door."

Mac whipped out his Swiss Army knife, hunkered down in front of the door knob, and got to work. A few seconds later he pushed it open.

"Wow," I said, totally impressed. "That was fast."

Mac preened. "Go on. I got you covered."

I slipped inside Pauley's room and quickly scanned the area. I wasn't exactly sure what I was looking for, but I needed to find some sort of clue in here.

Hey! Wait for me!

I chuckled and watched as Rex wiggled and jiggled and tried to squeeze his backside under the door. He looked up at me mid-wiggle and grinned his toothy grin.

Too many of the wife's cookies. She's a keeper. Yes, she is!

He finally pushed his bottom half under the door and scurried over to where I stood. I didn't mention the dent in his backside or the fact he was breathing hard.

"I'm not sure what I'm looking for," I whispered. "I just want to get a picture of how Pauley died."

Let's explore!

There was a three-drawer dresser pushed against one of the walls, a single bed exactly like the one in my room upstairs, and a wooden chair with a vinyl cushion in front of a TV tray. Perched on the TV tray was an actual record player. I walked over and marveled at the tiny black record inside. I'd seen one before, of course, but it had been in the museum.

Crazy by Patsy Cline.

A tiny TV sat on top of the dresser, and a broken-down recliner sat dejectedly in the middle of the room. I figured that was the chair Pauley sat in when he had his supposed stroke and either stood to get help and fell, or someone gave him a little extra shove.

86

If the latter was true, then that means Pauley had help with his stroke. No way could someone time it just right. I needed to find a clue to give to Detective Hackett so maybe something more could be done. If I could prove it may have been a suspicious death, the coroner would have to look into it more.

I waved my hand and slid open all three dresser drawers. Rex popped up from the first drawer.

Not much in here! Not at all.

Leaning over, I peered inside. Underwear, undershirts, and socks in top drawer. I carefully moved everything around but didn't see anything hidden. The next two drawers were the same...clothes but nothing hidden between them. No clues.

I slid the drawers closed with my mind and walked over to his desk. I didn't think he'd have much use for the desk anymore since he couldn't write. A couple items were strewn about the top, but nothing stood out. A drinking glass with a tall crazy straw was perched on the edge of the desk.

I frowned down at the glass. There was something odd about it.

"Rex, why would the glass be over here if Pauley didn't need to use the desk anymore to write?"

On it!

Rex jumped up on the chair, and I waved my hand to open the unseen drawer most desks had under the top. Rex jumped inside as I sat down on the metal folding chair.

We got pens, paperclips, and a roll of twenty-five cent stamps. Hey! Wonder if the wife could use this spool of thread?

"Focus, Rex."

Bingo, kid! I found something!

Rex was standing on top of a newspaper clipping looking pleased with himself. I pulled it out and scanned it. It was a newspaper article that ran when Pauley was shot in the line of duty. The article was dated August 16, 1976. Twelve years ago almost to the day.

"Officer Paul Ridgeway was recently shot in the line of duty after being called out to Gravestone Mental Hospital on the night of August 14, 1976. Gunshots were fired, and Officer Ridgeway took two bullets—but not before killing Dr. Melvin Stark, the lead psychiatrist at Gravestone Mental Hospital."

Whoa! What? Lexi, back that train up!

"I know! What the heck?"

Dr. Melvin Stark? Was this Dr. Stark's *dad*? Why had Pauley shot him? And more importantly, did *our* Dr. Stark know Pauley shot and killed his dad? But I knew the answer to that question. Of course our Dr. Stark knew. There'd be no way he couldn't know who shot and killed his father.

Keep reading, Lexi! Keep reading!

"Dr. Melvin Stark had come under recent scrutiny when allegations of misconduct were filed against him. Family members from three individual patients at the mental hospital reported the allegations. There's been no comment from Stark's wife or son, Jonathan. Jonathan is currently in his third year of college with plans to enroll in med school to follow in his father's footsteps."

That's a huge clue, kid. Good job!

I put the newspaper clipping back in the drawer and pushed back from the desk. Still reeling from what I'd just discovered, I was about to turn around when something on the floor caught my eye. A piece of paper was wedged between the back of the desk and the wall...the top portion sticking out.

"What's that?"

I reached down and yanked the paper out.

Lemme see. Lemme see.

Rex hopped out of the drawer and onto the desk. I set the piece of paper down on the desk so we could both see.

It was a postcard of the night shift. I recognized Dr. Stark, Nurse Shue, Stew, and Nikki. The other nurse in the picture I assumed was Nurse Noland. Two other aides I didn't recognize were also in the picture. The bottom of the postcard read, "Happy 4th of July from the night staff."

"This picture is two months old," I said. "Dr. Stark, Nurse Noland, and Nurse Shue are all smiling and laughing. Nothing looks out of place."

Lexi, Stew looks creepy. Creepy, I say!

I laughed. Stew was indeed staring all creepy-like at the camera. "I think that's just his resting bitch face."

Rex stood up on his hind legs and lifted his front paw up in the air. It took me a half second to realize he wanted me to give him a high-five.

It was the strangest high-five I'd ever given in my life.

"Why would Pauley have this postcard behind his desk?"

I flipped the card over and my heart lurched. There was a mass of squiggly lines written in pencil. I squinted at the lines, trying to figure out what it was. The more I studied the first squiggle line, the more I was sure it was a shaky lightning bolt.

"Rex, is this a lightning bolt?"

A lightning bolt? Hmmm...maybe.

The next shaky line was a vertical line with a long slash through it.

"What do you think this second squiggle line is?" I asked.

Hmm...maybe a "t" or "h"...maybe.

I put the postcard down and slid the desk back away from the wall. A tiny, sharpened-down pencil lay on the floor. I picked it up and tried not to gag at the teeth marks around the bottom of the number two pencil.

More treasure! I like it! I like it!

"It looks like Pauley gripped the pencil with his teeth and tried to write a message."

I picked the postcard back up, looked at the people, then flipped it back over to stare at the squiggled mess. Imagining myself in Pauley's shoes, I closed my eyes and thought about the people on the front cover and how I'd write their names.

My eyes flew open!

"Rex, it's not a lightning bolt. It's the letter 's'. Pauley didn't have complete control over the pencil since it was in his mouth, so of course it wouldn't be perfect."

I flipped the postcard back over and studied the faces.

I'd have to find out who the other aides were in the picture just to rule them out as suspects, but I was pretty sure Pauley had just narrowed down and confirmed my suspicions.

The three people I needed to press were Dr. Stark, Nurse Shue, and Stew. All three names started with the letter "s". I just couldn't be one hundred percent sure if the second letter was a "t" or an "h".

"I wonder why he didn't finishing writing out the full clue," I mused.

Had the killer been on to Pauley? What had he done to tip his hand? As far as I knew, Pauley couldn't speak recognizable words or write with his hands. The only thing he'd done the last day of his life was yell at people.

I shoved the postcard in the pocket of my uniform and hurried toward the door. I'd think about everything else later in my bedroom.

I was about to open the door when I felt my hairs stand up. I closed my eyes and sensed two males close by.

I opened the door and hissed at Mac. "You need to—"

"What're you doing out of your room?" Stew yelled.

I jerked back inside Pauley's room. I didn't want Stew to see me.

"I need a distraction," I whispered.

You need a rat? Did you say you need a rat, Lexi? Well, here I am!

I glanced down and my mouth dropped open. Rex was standing on his hind legs in the open doorway...brandishing a toothpick.

"Where did you get a toothpick?" I hissed.

But Rex didn't answer. Instead, he shoved the toothpick in his tiny rat mouth, ran up the wall opposite the hallway, and then raced across toward Stew. At the last minute before reaching Stew's side, Rex leaped off the wall, unclamped the toothpick mid-leap, and let out a rebel yell.

Time to stab me a Stew! Whoohoohoo!

Stew caught sight of the rat as it flew toward him. Unable to get his hands up in time to block his face, Rex landed with his front claws on top of Stew's head, his back claws scrambling on Stew's face to catch onto something solid. Rex finally pushed off Stew's nose and scrambled the rest of the way on top of a still-screaming Stew.

"You need to go," I said to Mac as I stepped out into the hallway.

Mac laughed. "I need to watch this."

A young, long-haired male I hadn't met strolled around the corner. He had a mop in one hand and pushed a pail on wheels with his feet. Hooked to his uniform was a Walkman. Foamy black headphones sat over his ears.

"Whoa, dude." The man pulled off the headphones and leaned on the mop. His speech was slow and classic stoner-like. "What's going on, man?"

"A rat!" Stew cried, still trying to fling Rex off his back. "I think it's stabbing me!"

"Cool, man. Let me see if I can help."

Knowing I couldn't pass up an opportunity like this, I glanced at the mop in the guy's hand. Even if it turned out Stew wasn't the killer, he was still a bad seed.

I concentrated on the mop, and it jerked out of the janitor's hand, hitting Stew on the side of the head.

"Dammit, Mark," Stew cried. "Watch what you're doing!"

92

"Sorry, dude. Like, I guess it just slipped."

Perplexed, Mark stared at the mop handle in his hand as Stew continued jumping around. I let the mop fly again, this time hitting Stew on the back.

"What the heck, Mark!" Stew cried. "Get away from me!"

"But, dude, I'm not—"

The mop hit Stew three more times on his back.

Mac was bent over at the waist, laughing so hard tears streamed from his eyes. Doors opened up and down the hall as people stepped out to see what was going on.

"I find out you had something to do with this, Mac," Stew yelled, "and you're a dead man!"

Stew pushed Mark aside and ran down the hallway, took a right at the end, and headed toward the nurses station. Nurse Shue happened to walk down the women's hallway at the exact same time.

Panicking that Nurse Shue had heard Stew's threat, I pushed Mac inside Pauley's room. Figuring if she didn't see Mac, maybe she'd think Stew was out of his mind. Which he obviously was. Nurse Shue looked at me with an arched eyebrow but didn't say anything...just kept walking toward the nurses station. One by one the doors closed and the people went back inside their rooms.

Mark stood in the hallway, still staring at his mop as Mac staggered out of Pauley's room still laughing. Mark gave his mop a quick shake. Something told me this guy liked his wacky tobacky a little too much.

A few seconds later Mark looked up at Mac and me, a glazed look in his eye. "Dudes. Like, I don't know what happened. It's like it was possessed."

"Well, that was the best entertainment I've had in months," Mac said. "I better get back to my room before Nurse Shue catches me out."

I didn't want to tell him I think she already had. Instead, I reached out and caught Mac's arm. "Should we be worried at Stew's threat?"

"Nah. He's all talk."

Mac gave me a wink and hurried down to his room, shutting the door silently behind him.

I turned back to Mark. He was still staring at his mop handle. "You better finish mopping before Nurse Shue comes back down this hallway."

Mark slowly turned his head my way. "Later, dude."

He slipped his headphones back on, pushed a button on the Walkman, and shuffled slowly down the hallway, carefully pushing the wheeled pail in front of him.

I grabbed one of the overstuffed laundry carts and headed toward the rec room. As I walked past the nurses station, Nurse Shue and Stew stopped talking and watched me.

"Did you check and make sure the list of names I gave you took their nightly medications?" Nurse Shue asked.

Since Gravestone Manor wasn't a typical nursing home, and the residents were fairly self-sufficient, they were able to track their own medicine intake. My job was to go down the list of names and just double check with them at night that they remembered to take their medication.

94

"Yes. The eight names I was given have all indicated to me they took their meds."

Nurse Shue nodded once. "Excellent."

I bumped my hip against the laundry cart and proceeded down to the laundry room. As far as I could tell, Dr. Stark had the right idea letting the patients be responsible for their own medical care, he just needed help in non-medical related areas, like letting the residents choose their own entertainment and eating times. For that matter, even where they ate. But I guess that was hind sight on my part since I knew what the future held for modern-day assisted living facilities. Right now, just out of the gate, I thought Dr. Stark was doing a fabulous thing. I just hoped for the residents' sake it didn't turn out Dr. Stark was the killer.

It was only ten o'clock, which meant I still had another two hours until midnight. I made use of my time by stealing a medical gown out of the tiny closet in the laundry room so I had something to sleep in. I also grabbed a toothbrush and some toothpaste while in there. I then stashed them in the tunnel so I could run down and get them after my shift.

Rex found me and reported in for his next assignment. That's pretty much how he said it, too. The rat was definitely tenacious in his job, but I sent him to my room to rest up. He'd had a long day, and I really didn't think there'd be anymore need of him tonight.

I hid out between the solarium and rec room trying to formulate a plan to sneak down into Dr. Stark's office during the afternoon hours and see what I could find. To my surprise, I only caught glimpses of Nurse Shue and Stew the rest of the night. I didn't see Dr. Stark, either. But I remembered someone saying he usually left around ten. So I wasn't shocked I didn't see him.

I was about to go out of my mind with boredom around eleven-thirty when a scream reverberated down the hallway into the solarium. I jerked up from the table where I'd been snoozing and sped down the hallway past the nurses station. I was shocked to see it was empty.

I was even more shocked to see Nurse Shue and Stew running down the men's hallway. What had they been doing? Checking on the residents? Why hadn't they asked me to do that?

I stopped in front of the door with the screaming, but was quickly pushed aside by Nurse Shue and Stew. A couple other doors along the women's hall had opened. I caught sight of Isabella and hurried over to her door.

"I wonder what's going on?" I said.

"It's just Mazie," Isabella said. "She's been forgetting more and more lately where she is, and even who we are. I'm not exactly sure what's wrong with her, but sometimes she gets so confused she just starts screaming."

Dementia? Alzheimer's?

"I heard that Dr. Stark may have to transfer her to another facility where she can get more specialized treatment," Isabella said.

Again, why hadn't he done that for Pauley? Pauley obviously needed more help than any other resident here.

It was midnight by the time Nurse Shue and Stew got Mazie calmed down and for everyone in the hall to get settled back into their rooms. Nurse Shue and I were heading

96

toward the nurses station, my eyes peeled to see where Stew had run off to.

The front door opened and another nurse walked in at about the same time an aide from second floor walked down the stairs. I gave him a nod then turned to Nurse Shue.

"Can I call it a night?" I asked.

Nurse Shue looked at me with hard eyes. "I heard Mac was out of his room tonight. Do you know anything about that?"

I shook my head. "I sure don't."

"According to Stew you were in the hallway with Mac. And I saw you in the hallway, too."

"Well, I heard a commotion and went to see what was going on." I gave her what I hoped was an innocent look.

"Stew said it looked like you came out of Paul Ridgeway's room. A room that is off limits."

Again I gave her a blank look. "No. I didn't come from inside that room."

"See that you don't find your way in there, either. That room is off limits according to Dr. Stark."

I bristled at her tone and decided to push the envelope a little. "I wanted to say I'm sorry about your friend Nurse Noland. I heard you two were close."

"Is that so?" Nurse Shue asked. "You were asking around about us?"

"No, no. I just asked someone what happened is all. They said not only had Nurse Noland supposedly fallen down a flight of stairs and died from a broken neck, but a couple nights later another resident here had a sudden stroke and had fallen over dead."

When she didn't say anything, I pressed on. "Don't you find that odd?"

"No. I don't," Nurse Shue said. "Nurse Noland had an unfortunate accident and fell down the stairs, while Paul Ridgeway—according to Nurse Wilson and Dr. Stark—had a stroke. Goodnight, Lexi."

Knowing when I was being dismissed, I gave her a small wave and slowly trudged up the first set of stairs. At the landing I turned and headed up the last set of stairs to the second floor. I glanced down and saw Nurse Shue watching me ascend the stairs.

Still no sign of Stew.

CHAPTER 11

Wake up! Wake up! It's bad! Bad, bad, bad!

I groaned and rolled over on my hideous cot. Every muscle in my body screamed in pain. How did people live today without at least memory foam on their beds?

Lexi! Up! Up!

I opened one eye and peeked down at the little rat running back and forth along the bed.

"What's up, Rex?"

Yes! Up! Up! You need to get up! Bad!

I bolted up, fear running through my stiff body.

"What's wrong? What's happened?"

A rapid knock on the door startled me.

"Lexi?" a voice hissed. "Dude, you awake? I need to get out of the hall."

I threw back the covers and flung open my door. Grabbing Billy by the sleeve, I hauled him inside and slammed the door shut.

"What's wrong?" I asked.

"I had to sneak up here. If I get caught, I could get in serious trouble."

"Fine. Fine." I motioned for him to hurry with his story. "What's wrong?"

"Henry and Isabella asked me to come up here and tell you that Mac..."

"That Mac what?" I practically screamed.

"Chill, he's not dead or anything."

I sucked in a breath and covered my hands over my mouth. Tears pricked my eyes.

"But it's not looking good for him," Billy went on.

"Start at the beginning," I demanded. "What happened?"

"Okay. So the one aide they have left on graveyard shift, I guess, like, he went into the rooms last night around two to check on the residents. And when he got to Mac's room, Mac was on the floor."

"Someone attacked him?"

Billy shrugged. "Nah. Nurse Wilson—the graveyard nurse—told Nurse Lohman this morning during shift change that he probably just fell out of bed."

Doubtful!

Yeah! Doubtful! Doubtful! Someone's going down! They don't call me Rex the Destroyer for nothing!

"This isn't like other nursing homes," Billy said. "These guys don't have to have special beds with rails or anything, so I guess I can see where he might have fallen."

"Can I see him?" I asked.

Billy shook his head. "They have him in the infirmary."

"That's the basement, right?" I asked.

"Yes. Downstairs in the basement," Billy said. "But not only is it super creepy down there. Like, unless you have authorization, aides like us can't really go down there."

Oh, yeah? Watch me!

Yeah! Watch us! We'll be down there so fast...they'll get whiplash! They won't know what hit 'em! I'll do the one-two punch.

I bit my lip to keep from smiling.

100

"Thanks for telling me about Mac," I said. "Do you think you can sneak back down without Nurse Shue or Stew catching you up here in the hallway?"

Billy nodded. "Yeah. They're probably still asleep or down the hall in the kitchen. I was able to sneak up because I said I was going to check on a couple of the old people since we just finished with breakfast."

I laid my hand on Billy's arm. "Thanks for coming up here to tell me. If you speak with Isabella and Henry, tell them I'm sorry about Mac."

Billy nodded and hurried out of my room, quietly shutting the door behind him.

Want me to check on him? I will. No one will know. No one will know.

"Yes, Rex. Please go down and at least check on him. I'm going to get changed and then make my way down. I'll take the hidden tunnel Mac showed me yesterday."

Okay! Wait here. I'll be right back.

Rex bolted across the room and after a few extra wiggles, finally squeezed his massive body under the door. I quickly threw off my gown and donned my white uniform. I decided to forgo the support hose. I didn't have time to wrestle into them. I put on my white scrunch-down socks and Sperry shoes.

After brushing my teeth, I attacked my hair. Three minutes later I gave up the useless attempt to tame the frizz and height, and finger-combed my way through as much as I could. I still didn't have need of the miniature Aqua Net hairspray. My hair wasn't going to move for another decade.

He's okay! He's okay! Dr. Stark is with him now.

101

I looked down at Rex. He was panting hard...his little chest heaving up and down.

"You okay?" I asked him.

Oh, yeah.

Pant.

Pant.

They don't call me...

Pant.

Pant.

Rex the Sprinter...

Pant.

Pant.

For nothing!

Pant.

Pant.

"Let's go then."

I shoved the cassette, gum, quarter, hairspray, and the four matches Mac gave me in my front pockets. "Go ahead of me, and let me know if the coast is clear."

Rex gave me a tiny salute and squeezed back under the door. I could have just closed my eyes and sensed if someone was in the hall, but I wanted to give Rex a job.

Coast clear. Coast clear. C'mon!

I yanked open my bedroom door and peered down the hallway. No one moved about. I quietly closed my door and sprinted down the hallway. When I neared the hidden passageway, I looked around again for good measure. Seeing no one, I waved my hand in front of the door so it would open, dashed inside, and then closed the door behind me.

Darkness engulfed me.

I'd recently started practicing spells so I wouldn't have to rely solely on my powers of movement and sensing. The first spell I learned was how to make a glow globe. Or at least that was what it was *supposed* to be. I somehow got the spell wrong and could now only conjure up a glitter globe...and they were never the same color.

With a flick of my wrist, I released my version of the glow globe into the air. A pink, circular globe about four inches in diameter appeared overhead. The light from the globe had a soft, pale shine...which wouldn't be so bad if that was all it did. Unfortunately, with my globe, about every five seconds little puffs of glitter shot into the air. The puffed glitter shimmered, sparkled, and danced midair before quickly fading into nothing. Luckily, no residual glitter was left behind.

Something told me if I ever found a way to give voice to the little puffed glitter, it would sound like mischievous elves running through the woods, screaming and laughing as they tried to evade capture.

Eek! What is that? I'm not gonna be pink, am I? Pink sparkles isn't exactly my color.

I glanced down at Rex, who was thoroughly examining his body for glitter—in between his paws, his tail, his fur.

"No you aren't gonna be pink," I hissed. "Let's go."

I scrambled down the stairs, using the soft glow from the globe so I didn't fall. When I reached the first floor, I carefully shuffled past the closed door and started down the last of the curved stairs until I reached the bottom. With a final flick of my wrist, the globe popped, and the tunnel went dark.

I closed my eyes and tried to sense if anyone else was in the basement, but something was off. It was like I felt people all around.

"Rex, can you find Mac from here?" I asked.

Hold on. Hold on.

I closed my eyes—sort of a ridiculous thing to do since I was standing in complete darkness—and focused on my breathing. Focused on centering myself.

Coast clear. No more Doc around.

"Good. Stick close and keep your eyes open."

I physically cracked the door just wide enough to see out. When I didn't see any movement, I opened the door wider and stuck my head out to get the lay of the land.

To the right of me, way down toward the end of the darkened, crumbling hallway was the stairs that led up to the first floor. A blue tarp with yellow tape marked off the rest of the hallway to the right of the stairs. A "Do Not Enter" sign hung down from the ceiling in front of the tarp. I remembered Dr. Stark telling me that the west wing was closed off down here. It was too damaged. Which was really saying something, because the condition of the basement's east wing wasn't all that great.

Obviously the building codes in this time period were a little more lax than they were in modern times.

I stepped out from inside the tunnel, swiped my hand to close the door, and stood in the middle of the hallway. There were six doors total—three on either side of the hallway. Two of the doors had small windows in them. One lone door at the end of the east wing hallway had an old Boiler Room sign

104

stuck to it. An even bigger sign underneath the Boiler Room sign said "Do Not Enter."

Mac in middle rooms.

"Okay," I whispered. "But I want to see if there's anything I might be able to pick up on in the other rooms."

I decided to start at the top of the hallway by the stairs and work my way down to the boiler room and hidden passageway. An overhead light popped and fizzled as I scurried up the passageway.

When I reached the staircase, I waved my hand to open the metal door to my left. No way was I touching the rusted doorknob. The door creaked open, and a chill ran down my spine. The rooms down here were playing havoc with my sensing ability. I could swear I felt the presence of three different people around me.

I slowly stepped inside the dank, dark room. I didn't want to conjure up a light globe just in case I got caught snooping, so I had to make do with what light I was given. There was a tiny window about twelve feet high, but it barely let in enough sunlight to see. Years of grime and neglect made it nearly impossible for the rays to penetrate. Still, there was enough of a glow that I could see.

And I wish I hadn't.

The plastered walls were crumbling and falling down. A lone, metal gurney that looked like it was from the late eighteen hundreds sat precariously in the middle of the room, one wheel broken off.

There were words and drawings scrawled all over the walls. I stepped closer to see if I could make anything out. I assumed the names were of patients living in the room when it was still an asylum. There were disturbing drawings of animals with all different body parts and of humans with missing limbs. I backed up so quickly, I nearly tripped over my feet. I didn't want to look any closer.

Rex and I stumbled out of the room and went across the hall. This door had a small window in the middle of the peeled metal door. Upon closer inspection, the glass was no longer in the frame. A sudden chill passed over my face, and my pulse quickened. There was no reason for the room to be about twenty degrees colder inside. I closed my eyes and could sense something was off. While there wasn't a person inside per se, the room had an ominous feel that honestly terrified me.

"Just look inside," I whispered to myself. "You can do it, Lexi. You're a Howe."

I told myself this was probably a thousand times nicer than what they kept my too-many-greats-to-remember grandmother in when they jailed her for being a witch. If she could endure that kind of treatment, the least I could do is have the courage to stick my head inside the abandoned room.

But I had this mental image of a grasping hand reaching through the open space...or a demonic face popping up right as I went to peer inside. No way could I lie to myself and say I wasn't scared. I'd battled a lot of bad guys over the last year...some human, some supernatural...some I'm not sure how to classify.

What I knew for certain was that evil existed, and there was something about the downstairs dungeon that gave me the willies. Like I could feel and sense the oppression and horror and pain still etched in the walls.

"Rex, whaddya say you go in and take a look around?" I suggested.

Scaredy cat! Chicken! Scaredy witch!

I rolled my eyes. "Whatever. Just get in there."

They don't call me Rex the Fearless for nothing!

I heard a cough from another room down the hallway. A hysterical laugh bubbled up inside me, and I had to clamp down on it before it escaped.

"Never mind," I said. "Let's go see Mac."

I didn't care what it said about me, I couldn't bring myself to look inside the open window *or* send Rex inside.

Good! Good! Rex the Fearless may have been a stretch.

Following Rex, I crossed the hallway and stood in front of another door—this one wooden with a glass window.

I leaned up on my tiptoes and peeked inside. Mac was in a single cot like the one I had in my room, with an open cot on either side of him. I couldn't see what the other side of the room looked like, so I had no idea if anyone else was in there. Again, it felt packed in the room.

"Were any other residents in there?" I asked.

Nope. Just Mac.

I swung my hand in front of the door and it slid open effortlessly. Mac turned his head and gave me a wobbly smile when he saw me. Rex and I rushed inside, and I gently closed the door.

"Hey, Mac."

I took in the rest of the room as we hurried over to him. Three more cots were on the opposite side of the room, with a small desk at the end of one row. I assumed that was where the nurse sat and watched over the patients.

"Where's your nurse?" I asked.

Mac grunted. "Dr. Stark says he thinks I fell out of bed. No need for a nurse."

"Does he now? And what do you think?"

"Well, Dr. Stark admits my heartbeat is a little elevated, I have a splitting headache, I'm a little dizzy when I sit up, and I feel like I've swallowed a bag of cotton balls." Mac looked me in the eyes. "I think I was drugged or something."

"Did you tell Dr. Stark that?" I asked.

"Yes." Mac frowned. "He *did* check my arms and fingers, and he said he didn't see any puncture wounds."

I frowned at his words. Checking fingers and arms was fine, but what about the other five hundred places on the body? Did Dr. Stark just check the obvious arms because he was humoring Mac or because he knew where the injection site actually was and didn't want Mac to discover the puncture wound for himself?

"How would someone have gotten into your room and injected you without you knowing?" I asked.

Mac shrugged. "The only thing I can think of is that they waited until my sleeping pill took effect."

"You take a sleeping pill? Who would know that?"

"All the nurses on staff, Dr. Stark, and since I take the sleeping pill at night, Stew would know. He's my person that comes in and asks if I've taken everything at night."

"Darn. I was hoping maybe that would be a clue as to who knew, but it sounds like everyone did."

108

Mac nodded. "Yes. Dr. Stark allows us to keep track of our own medication as long as we can. But we do have to provide him and the nurses with a list of said medications. So all of them would have known, and Stew knew because sometimes I joke about finally getting a good night's sleep if he's in my room when I'm taking it. I'm sorry I couldn't help you out there."

"Oh, Mac, it's okay. I just thought maybe I could have gotten a clue, but it's not a big deal. We'll figure it out a different way."

"We do know one thing," Mac said with a twinkle in his eye. "I think since I didn't die, we can rule out it's a ghost or a curse doing the killing." He looked at me with a steady, unwavering gaze. "And that's what this is, right? Murder. Someone murdered Nurse Noland and my friend, Pauley?"

I nodded. "Yes. And I believe now they've tried to kill you."

"Who?"

I shrugged. "I'm not exactly sure yet. I have some ideas, but nothing concrete. I think I've narrowed it down to three people."

"Well, Stew did say he would kill me if he got a chance," Mac volunteered. "And he hated Nurse Noland because she was about to fire him. But why Pauley? For that matter, why would *anyone* want to hurt Pauley?"

I sat down on the edge of a vacant bed next to him, while Rex scurried up the bed frame to sit next to me. If Mac thought it odd a rat was sitting next to me, he didn't say anything.

"What do you know about when Pauley was shot?" I asked. "The reason he had to leave the force?"

"Not a whole lot," Mac admitted. "I knew he was due to retire not too long after he'd been shot, but otherwise he was pretty private about the whole thing. He just said one night he had to make a judgment call, and it was a call that haunted him daily."

"Mac, I found a newspaper clipping in his room. It talked about the shooting. He was shot in August of nineteen seventy-six. Here at this facility. Only it wasn't a nursing home back then, it was a mental hospital. Pauley was called out here for some reason, and the person he shot and killed was Dr. Melvin Stark, a psychiatrist for the mental hospital."

Mac gasped. "Dr. Stark? Like *our* Dr. Stark?"

"Well, since it was twelve years ago, and our Dr. Stark's first name is Jonathan, I'm venturing it was our Dr. Stark's *dad*."

Mac gave a sheepish laugh. "Oh, yeah. I'm still a little foggy."

"No problem. From what I gathered, there were some pretty serious allegations against Dr. Stark right before he died." I leaned over and touched Mac's arm. "I'm going into town today before I clock in this afternoon to talk with Judy, the graveyard aide who found Pauley. See if she can tell me anything about the night Pauley died. What she remembers."

"Because if it *is* Dr. Stark who's the killer, you think maybe he killed Pauley to get back at him? But why kill Nurse Noland? And why try and kill me?"

"Again, I have some theories." I stood up and started to pace. "I think maybe Dr. Stark could be the killer, but he may

110

also have an accomplice. I know that around eleven-thirty last night, when another resident started having difficulties, Nurse Shue and Stew were both coming from your hallway. Maybe one of them is helping Dr. Stark."

"This is huge," Mac said. "How can you prove it, though?"

"I don't know," I said honestly. "Other than to pick the brain of this Judy girl. Maybe she saw something and doesn't remember."

Mac struggled to sit up. "I wish I could go with you. This isn't the kind of thing a girl should do alone."

I grinned at him. I couldn't help it. I knew it was the era he grew up in, thinking chicks couldn't hold their own...so I didn't hold it against him. "I'll be careful. I promise."

"I don't have my duct tape or Swiss Army knife on me," Mac said. "If I did, I'd give them to you."

I leaned over and gave him a hug. "I still have a couple matches, I think." I dug down in my pocket and handed him the rest of my gum. "Keep this safe for me."

"I will. Because like I said, you never know when a stick of gum will come in handy."

CHAPTER 12

I poked my head out the door to make sure the coast was clear before stepping out into the hallway. I gently closed the door behind me and leaned against it.

"I need you to stay here, Rex, and keep an eye on things. Right now, Dr. Stark is here, and both Nurse Shue and Stew are on the second floor. I need you to keep an eye out for them and monitor their every move."

Aye aye, Captain. As you command.

I closed my eyes and grounded myself to see if I could sense where Dr. Stark was. I was tempted to sneak into his office and see if I could find a clue. I mean, it's not like I thought he'd leave a bottle of whatever drug he used to zap Mac with, but there might be something I could use to prove his guilt.

I let out a frustrated sigh when hordes of weakened energies washed over me. There were too many emotions and leftover imprints of tortured souls down in the dungeon for me to get a true reading of where someone might be.

"Rex, go see if Nurse Lohman is behind the nurses station."

Rex stood up on his hind legs, clicked them together, and took off up the stairs. I crept slowly down the hallway in the opposite direction toward what I presumed was Dr. Stark's office. There were only two other rooms—except for the boiler room door—that was left to explore in the east wing.

I was about to push Dr. Stark's door open with a swipe of my hand when Rex somersaulted down the stairs, his little

112

body splatting against the wall. He got up, shook himself, and turned toward me.

Hide! Hide! He's coming!

Pushing Dr. Stark's door open, I leaped over the threshold and looked around for a place to hide. There were only two bulky items in the room: his desk and a tall, metal storage container.

I yanked open the double doors of the storage unit. It was a small closet. There were two long lab coats, an umbrella, and a set of casual clothes hanging on a wire hanger. I jumped inside and slid my hand backward to close the door. Inhaling slowly, I tried to stabilize my breathing. Counting to five slowly, I centered myself...and nearly jumped out of my skin when the office door slammed shut. A few seconds later I heard wheels screech, springs rock, and a fist slam down on the metal desk.

Obviously the doc's not having a good day.

"Well, Dad, it's been twelve years," Dr. Stark said bitterly. "Twelve years and it still haunts me."

There was a knock on the door.

"What?" Dr. Stark growled.

"I'm sorry to bother you, Dr. Stark, but you're needed again upstairs."

I recognized Nurse Lohman's voice.

"I'll be right there," Dr. Stark said.

"Of course, doctor."

The door closed quietly, and I waited impatiently for Dr. Stark to leave. A drawer closed, and then finally the click of his office door sounded. I waited another thirty seconds just for good measure.

He's gone! He's gone. C'mon out!

I stepped carefully out of the metal closet and strolled over to Dr. Stark's desk. The largest, chunkiest computer I'd ever seen in my life took up practically the whole desk. There was no way the screen was more than six inches tall. I wasn't sure how he saw anything on it.

I picked up the only picture frame in the room. It was a picture of a younger Dr. Stark—maybe high school—with his arm around a man who looked exactly like him. The other Dr. Stark. They were both laughing. I put the picture back where it was, and Rex and I silently walked into the hallway.

A sudden chill ran down me, and the hairs on my arm stood up. I had a feeling I wasn't alone down here, and it was more than just Mac in the infirmary. Determined to try and block out the myriad energies rushing me, I closed my eyes and concentrated on pushing aside everything but Mac's presence. When I had a sense of him, I let my mind open up to the other presence I thought I felt in the basement.

Nothing.

Well, not exactly nothing, just a faint tapping at the back of my brain, like someone just out of reach. I couldn't be certain, but I felt like it was a female.

Was Nurse Lohman coming back down the stairs? Not waiting to find out, I pushed open the secret door and Rex and I stepped inside. Flicking my wrist, I sent up a light globe. This time it was red.

I was about to head up the steps when something caught my eye. Bringing the globe down to ground level, I squatted for a closer look at the stain on the floor. I hadn't noticed it before on my journey down because I'd

114

extinguished the light too soon. The stain was butted up against the side of the stone wall and floor, almost in a crevice.

"Rex, can you check and make sure the coast is clear and Nurse Shue or Stew aren't in the kitchen making breakfast on the second floor?"

On it! You can count on me!

I squinted down at the stain again. I was pretty sure it was blood. Of course, that didn't mean it was recent. It could have been here for decades. I remembered reading once where scientists gathered blood from a tool used in Mesopotamia.

Regardless, it was worth noting for Detective Hackett. I may not know exactly how the blood got in the tunnel, but if it meant he was able to come back with a team and extract the blood, it might make the killer just nervous enough to twitch.

And I'd see the twitch.

I had to. While I technically still had five days to solve the crime, I was anxious to get out of this location. Seven days was the maximum amount of time the Agency of Paranormal Peculiarities gave us to work a cold case. Seven days. After that we were pulled back into our own time period.

I jogged up the stairs and paused at the top of the second-floor landing. I looked around but didn't see any blood up here. Waving my hand, the red glitter globe popped, and I was again plunged into darkness.

Coast clear! Run for it!

I motioned my hand backward and the door slid open. Sticking my head out, I double checked to make sure Rex was right. When I didn't see or sense anyone, I hopped out into the hallway. Closing the tunnel door, Rex and I took off at breakneck speed.

"I'm going to change my clothes real quick then call Nikki for a ride," I said. "I should be back here around one or so."

Count on me to snoop. They don't call me Rex the Nosey for nothing!

I hurried into my room and changed into the only non-uniformed clothes I had—the Z. Cavaricci jeans and Guess sweatshirt. Transferring the mini Aqua Net hairspray, cassette, postcard clue from last night, and the quarter from my uniform to my jean pocket, I picked up Nikki's phone number and hurried out of my room and down the stairs. At the landing between the first and second floor, I bent down to see if Nurse Lohman was at the counter. She was, but she was at the filing cabinet...which meant her back was to me.

Tiptoeing down the stairs, I knew I was going to have to say something before I opened the door to go outside, I just didn't know what. I'd just put my hand on the door when Nurse Lohman's voice rang out. "Good morning. Going out?"

I plastered a smile on my face and turned around. "Yes. I need to run into town real quick and pick up a few things."

"Have a nice afternoon."

With a half-hearted wave, I yanked open the door and stumbled outside. The glare of the morning sun made me squint and pause in my steps.

Geez, one full day inside these walls, and I'm squinting in the sun like a vampire.

I walked toward the payphone and dug out my quarter. This was something I *had* studied up on...how to use a payphone. Mainly because my first time-travel job took me back to nineteen seventy-three, and I had to use one then, too. It had been cheaper back then to call, more like ten cents, but I figured the mechanism of working the phone was still the same.

And I was glad to see I was wrong.

This payphone had numbers I could just push down on, which was great. I could do that. The first time I used a payphone, it had these circles around the numbers, and I had to insert my finger in the hole and loop the number over until it hit a metal stopper. It took me three tries just to do it. My finger kept slipping out of the hole and the blasted dial would go back to the beginning number.

But I didn't need to worry about that now. Fifteen years had improved the payphone to where you could push on the number, but it also cost the consumer more money. That was an inflated price I didn't mind paying.

I pulled out Nikki's number, inserted the quarter, and dialed. A few rings later Nikki picked up.

"Hello?"

"Hi. Nikki?"

"Like, that's me!"

I laughed. "It's Lexi. Over at Gravestone Manor. I was hoping you could do me a favor?"

"Sure. Whaddya need?"

I informed her about Mac and asked if she knew Judy who had worked the graveyard shift. When she said she did, I asked her to come pick me up and go with me to pay Judy a visit.

Twenty minutes later, her lime green Pinto chugged down the road. Halfway down the Gravestone Manor driveway, there was an offshoot that led you to the back of the nursing home. That was where the workers parked. But Nikki bypassed that driveway as I ran down the stairs and waited out front.

I opened the passenger door, dropped down into the seat, and shut the door. Or at least I tried to. I wasn't prepared for the weight of the long door. Unfortunately, I couldn't just wave my hand to shut it. Using two hands, I finally managed to pull the door closed.

"Whoa," I said, taking in the interior of the car. The steering wheel, seats, and even flooring were lime green. "The whole car is lime green." I ran my foot over the lime green and brown stained carpet on my floorboard. "Is this that shag carpet stuff?"

Nikki laughed. "Not quite. And, yeah, everything is lime green. It's not, like, the car I wanted, but it's the car I could afford."

"Don't sweat it. It's a cool car." It sounded like a lie even to my own ears. The car was hideous.

"So, like, I called Judy and asked if we could come over. She was *really* freaked when I told her about Mac. She's convinced it's a ghost."

Doubtful.

118

I settled back as we headed toward town. I grew up about fifty miles north of River Springs, so I wasn't too worried about running into anyone I might recognize from this time period.

Nikki jabbed her pink fingernail over the black buttons on the radio. "I have both AM and FM stations. So I'm sure we can find something." She kept clicking at the black buttons, pressing so hard I was afraid her fingers would snap.

"That looks dangerous," I mused.

Nikki's eyes grew wide. "Do you have one of them fancy radios that have, like, the cassette player built in? Is that why you carry around your cassette tape?"

"I don't, but my mom does." I just hoped she didn't ask me what kind of car it was, because I couldn't remember what it was my mom told me she drove as a teenager.

"Judy lives in a pretty cool house between Water and Mississippi." Nikki laughed self-consciously. "I forgot, like, you probably don't even know where that is."

CHAPTER 13

I actually *did* know where that was. It was about three blocks up from where I lived on the historic town square. Judy lived in a section of town I coveted.

Nikki pulled up in front of a humongous white Victorian. Six green and white pillars held up the pitched roof of the wraparound porch. The large turret on the right-hand side of the house boasted three green windows with ornate beveled glass. I could tell those windows were original to the house.

I tried not to gawk as Nikki and I walked up the wooden stairs onto the porch, but I couldn't help myself. I'd always loved big, old homes like these.

Nikki knocked on the door, and I heard a woman's voice ask someone named Tina to open the door. A few seconds later we were still standing on the porch. Nikki knocked again, and again a voice yelled for Tina to answer the door.

I looked at Nikki and she shrugged. She was getting ready to knock again when the door swung open and an exasperated middle-aged woman stood in the doorway with a laundry basket perched on her hip.

"I'm so sorry." She backed up so we could enter. "I told Tina to answer the door." Judy actually looked into another room and yelled that last part out.

A teenage girl, her back to us watching a big-box TV, didn't even budge. That is, until a commercial came on. Then she whipped her head around, and I barely contained my gasp. I thought my hairdo was hideous. This girl had one side of her hair slicked all the way over to the other side of her

120

head, and a limp ponytail stuck out from the side of her skull right above the ear. A huge, blue hooped earring hung from her ear. She jumped to her feet and stood with her hands on her hips. I could barely tell where one part of her started and the other part ended. She had on stone-washed jeans, a dark blue crop top, and the same colored stone-washed jean jacket.

"Mom, like, Adam Curry was on. I couldn't *not* watch!"

Nikki nodded her own frizzy hair, the bangs barely moving. "That Adam Curry. He has the most *amazing* hair!"

The girl perked up. "I know, right. Like, his hair is *so* bad!"

I frowned. "I thought you said it was amazing?"

The teenaged Tina and Nikki busted out laughing.

"Like, where's the square from?" Tina asked as she made a square in the air with her fingers.

"That's enough, Tina Marie," Judy said. "Come get your clothes and put them away."

The girl's eyes widened and she spun back to the TV and plopped down on the floor. "In a minute, Mom. I've been waiting *all day* for this new video!"

Judy sighed and put the basket of clothes down next to the oak staircase. Without a word she gestured for us to follow her.

"Only one more week until school starts," Judy said. "It can't come fast enough. Girl watches MTV nonstop. Nothing but music videos all day."

I smiled but said nothing. As far as I knew, MTV was now a reality station and not a music station. Bet Tina would apoplexy over that bit of news.

Judy motioned for us to sit down at the oak table. "Can I get you something to drink?"

Nikki and I both shook our heads. Nikki introduced me, and I got straight to the point. "Judy, last night someone tried to hurt Mac."

"I'm so sorry to hear that," Judy said. "But I know for a fact something awful is happening out there. That's why I had to quit."

"What do you mean you know for a fact?" I asked.

Judy pursed her lips together before answering. "I'll tell you the same thing I told the detective yesterday when he came to ask me questions. On the night that Pauley died, something weird happened to me."

Nikki sat up straighter in her chair. "Like what?"

"I usually keep to the same routine every night," Judy said. "I clock in and go straight to the laundry room. There are always at least four carts of laundry to do. Two from women's hallway and two from men's. Each cart does two loads. So that night I did the first two women's carts like I always do, which took up all four washing machines. While they were washing, I went to check on the women in their rooms. Make sure everything was okay, ya know?"

Nikki and I nodded.

"On my way back from checking on all the women," Judy continued, "I stopped and talked with Nurse Wilson. We talked for a little bit, then I went to put the women's laundry in the dryer and start the men's."

Judy suddenly shivered, and I covered her arm with my hand. "I know this is probably hard, but it could really help Mac."

122

Judy nodded. "When I stepped into the laundry room, it was a complete disaster. The two men's carts were overturned. Clothes and bedsheets were strewn around the room. It was a mess. I put the women's clothes into the dryer and then started to pick up the men's scattered laundry, and that's when I saw it."

"Saw what?" Nikki and I asked at the same time.

"Someone had written the words 'cursed' and 'leave now' on the table! And I'm pretty dang sure it was the ghost!"

I wasn't sure how to explain to Judy that I knew for a fact a ghost couldn't pick up a pen and write. So obviously it couldn't be a ghost.

"Could you tell if it was a man's writing or a woman's writing?" When Judy looked ready to argue with me, I amended my question. "I mean, could you tell by the writing if it was a man or woman ghost?"

Judy gasped. "I didn't even think of that! I didn't pay that much attention. It scared me so badly I couldn't even think. I ran out of the room to go get Nurse Wilson."

"So Nurse Wilson saw the destruction and writing?" I asked.

"Well, that's the even freakier part. When I brought Nurse Wilson in to show her the mess, all the clothes were back up off the floor and in the carts."

"No way!" Nikki exclaimed. "That *is* freaky!"

"And the words?" I asked.

"They were scratched out," Judy said.

Of course they were. Because they were written by a human, not a supernatural.

"Nurse Wilson told me to go check on the men's hallway, and that's when I found Pauley."

Tears fell from Judy's eyes. She quickly wiped them away, leaned over, and pulled a washcloth from the laundry basket. Dabbing at the corners of her eyes, she sniffed.

"Did you notice anything off about his room?" I asked. "Did it look disheveled or anything out of place?"

Judy shrugged and shook her head. "Not really. I mean, not that I could tell."

"What about the history of Gravestone Manor?" I asked. "Do either of you know why the mental hospital closed in nineteen seventy-six?"

Nikki giggled. "Well, considering, like, I was just a kid, I have no idea. Maybe they didn't have any more patients out there?"

"I don't know, either," Judy said. "I moved Tina and me out here a couple years ago from Maryville. So I'm still relatively new to the area."

"Hey," Nikki said, "maybe my mom would know. I'll ask her when I get home and tell you what she says when I get to work tonight."

"That would be great, thanks."

While I knew bits and pieces, I really needed someone to fill in all the gaps for me...since Google wasn't an option.

"Well, I guess we should go." I stood up and stuck my hand out to Judy. "Thank you for talking with us today. I don't know what exactly is going on out at Gravestone Manor, but I plan on figuring it out. I don't want Mac to have to look over his shoulder every day."

Judy walked us to the door. I said goodbye to Tina, but if she heard, she never let on.

"Nikki, can you do me one more favor?" I asked when we settled down in her Pinto. "Can you take me to the police station? I'd like to talk with Detective Hackett if I could."

"Sure. Hey, then afterward, like, how about we go have a Frito pie over at Frosty Freeze?"

I grimaced. "Oh, I really don't have—"

"My treat! I love those things. Have you ever had one?"

I laughed. "No. I can honestly say I haven't."

"Like, you're gonna *love* it. They open a little bag of Frito corn chips, add chili and cheese, and then you eat it right out of the bag. Totally cool."

"Sounds righteous," I said.

CHAPTER 14

The police station was running full force when we stepped through the front doors. It always surprised me how lax security was pre-9/11. No one frisked me, had me walk three times through the same metal detector, then an x-ray machine, then wand me again. This was just a simple walk in and talk to someone.

"Can I help you?"

I smiled across the front desk at a middle-aged woman with red-framed glasses so huge they practically swallowed her whole face.

"We'd like to see Detective Hackett. My name is Lexi Howe. I'm from Gravestone Manor, and I have some information for him."

"One moment please." She picked up a tan, press-button phone with six light-up buttons at the bottom. She pushed a couple numbers, spoke into the phone, then glanced back up at me. "Detective Hackett said he'll be right with you. Take a seat until he calls you back, please."

Nikki and I found two empty chairs and waited for Detective Hackett. Luckily we didn't have to wait too long, and a few minutes later he motioned for us to follow him back.

He led us through the center of the station. There were a handful of cops scattered around the room, some on typewriters working on forms and some talking with citizens. It was loud and active. It was comforting to know police stations hadn't changed much over the years. Better electronics, beefier security...but the overall function was still the same.

"Right through here, ladies," Detective Hackett said.

He steered us into his private office. It was a small room that barely fit his wooden desk and chair and two plastic chairs for guests. The walls were white and bare. He did have a photograph on his desk, but I couldn't see who or what it was. Overall, just like at the former insane asylum...if I had to spend too much time in the room, I'd go crazy.

"Now, what can I do for you, Ms. Howe?" Detective Hackett asked.

"There's been a lot going on at Gravestone the last twenty-four hours I believe you should know about," I said.

"Is that right?"

I could see Detective Hackett was seriously weighing what I'd just said...just as carefully as he was weighing what he should say next. Before I could jump in and explain, he picked up the phone on his desk and spoke to someone on the other end. Almost immediately the door opened and Detective Seaver poked in his head.

Nikki visibly perked up as Detective Hackett turned to Nikki.

"I believe you spoke with Detective Seaver the other day," he said. "Would you mind going with him while I visit with Ms. Howe?"

Nikki grinned and hopped up out of her chair. "Like, totally."

I took that to mean she was okay with it...seeing as how she all but ran out of the room.

"That should give us a chance to speak freely," Detective Hackett said.

In the other time traveling cases I'd been involved in, usually I went to great lengths and jumped through a ton of hoops to get the cops to take me seriously. Not that it mattered. I almost always ended up trampling on top of the local cops to get my bad guy. Not that I cared...I had a handler. Someone to come in from the Agency of Paranormal Peculiarities and clean up the mess I made. It would be nice if I didn't have to do that this time.

"How about you tell me everything you have so far?" he said.

"Just like that?" I couldn't help the snark. I wasn't used to cops giving me the benefit of the doubt.

"Just like that," Detective Hackett said. "Because right now, I'm getting pressure to close the file on Nurse Noland and conclude there was no foul play. That the ruling of accidental death stands. And unless I hear something different from the coroner, it looks like Paul Ridgeway's death will conclude he had a stroke, which caused him to fall and hit his head on the floor."

Now I understood why he was so eager to hear what I had to say. He needed a lifeline. Something to connect these two murders. "I'll start with what happened this morning. Mac, the guy who told you about Paul Ridgeway, was attacked last night. Now, the nursing home will officially tell you he fell out of bed, but I don't believe that, and neither does Mac. We think he was drugged or something. We aren't sure exactly what. I feel you need to know this in case it helps

128

sway you to dig deeper into to the two deaths that have occurred over the last week."

Detective Hackett held up his hand. "I've dedicated nearly thirty years of my life to law enforcement. I'm a pretty good judge of character, and my gut tells me something is off. And not just because Pauley was one of our own."

I nodded. "But you can't do anything further until you hear what the coroner says. I understand."

And that must be how it ended. The coroner must have agreed with the nursing home and declared it a stroke, and Detective Hackett spent the rest of his years arguing there was more to the story.

"As I'm sure you're aware," Detective Hackett said, "I cannot discuss anything relevant to this case as it is still officially ongoing. However, you're free to speak with me and tell me whatever it is you think I need to know."

"Perfect. Let me tell you what I've uncovered," I said. "I'm sure it won't be much different from what you already know. I know that Nurse Noland died sometime during the hours of midnight and two o'clock in the morning. She supposedly went downstairs to the basement to get medication she wasn't supposed to and tripped and fell down the stairs, thereby breaking her neck."

Detective Hackett nodded. "That is correct."

"I've put together a list of suspects and motives for her death."

Detective Hackett chuckled. "Have you now? Okay. Keep talking."

"I know that Pauley Ridgeway died just two nights later. The nurse on staff and Dr. Stark both believe he had a stroke.

It also looks like he fell and hit his head when he tried to get out of his chair."

"And I assume you have suspects and motives for his death, too?"

"I do. But first, are you aware that Dr. Stark and Nurse Noland were seeing each other?"

I saw the look of surprise flash in his eyes. "No."

"Mac is the one that told me he saw them kissing. Awhile back, Dr. Stark made him promise not to tell anyone. Mac told me he didn't even tell you. I thought you should know."

"Dr. Stark didn't volunteer the information, either."

I snorted. "He didn't volunteer it because technically they broke up a day or two before Nurse Noland died."

I let the ominous meaning hang in the air.

"Also, I know that Dr. Stark's dad, Dr. Melvin Stark, was shot and killed at Gravestone in nineteen seventy-six when it was a mental hospital. And as I'm sure *you* know, it was Paul Ridgeway who did the shooting."

Detective Hackett sighed. "Which is why I'm having a hard time with the whole coincidence thing. However, maybe I can stall for a little more time with the new angle of a relationship gone bad. Anything else?"

"I was thinking maybe Dr. Stark was worried that Mac would talk to the police about the on again-off again relationship with Nurse Noland, and so he decided to take matters into his own hands."

"There's only one problem with that," Detective Hackett said. "For both Nurse Noland's death and Pauley's death, Dr. Stark was not around."

I nodded. "Nor was he around last night when Mac was attacked. Supposedly."

Detective Hackett arched a brow. "What does that mean?"

"I'll tell you in a minute when I get to my other big news."

Detective Hackett chuckled. "Continue."

"I have a motive for Stew Rodgers to kill Nurse Noland, but not to kill Pauley. I was also standing not two feet from Stew last night when he threatened to kill Mac."

Detective Hackett's eyebrows rose. "You don't say? Perhaps I'll be spending a little more time out at Gravestone Manor yet."

I smiled. "That's not even the best part. Now, admittedly, Nurse Shue's motive to kill Nurse Noland and Pauley and harm Mac is my weakest. She could have killed Nurse Noland to get her job, but again I have no idea as to why she'd kill Pauley. Or why she'd kill Mac for that matter."

"But thanks to you I have new leads to follow up on," Detective Hackett said, "and I'm going to use them."

"One more big thing," I said.

Detective Hackett shook his head. "I need to see about putting you on the payroll. You've gotten more information in twenty-four hours than I've gotten in six days."

I grinned and lifted one shoulder. "I enjoy snooping."

Detective Hackett sat back in his chair and rested his hands over his stomach. "Okay. What's your big announcement?"

"I think I found blood in a secret tunnel."

Detective Hackett jerked upright in his chair. "What? What secret tunnel? What blood?"

"Mac showed me a hidden passageway yesterday. I've been traveling it to do some snooping. When I looked around in the tunnel on the ground floor—the basement—I found what looks to be a small smattering of blood. Of course, I don't know if it's a clue or not as to Nurse Noland's death, but it couldn't hurt to check it out just in case."

Detective Hackett didn't say anything for a few seconds. I could see he was pulling everything over in his head. "All this extra information *and* possible blood splatter in a semi-restricted area. I may be able to argue for a search warrant to check for DNA. It might take a few weeks to get the results back from the tests, which would allow me to keep an eye on everything, too."

I wasn't about to tell him I couldn't wait around long enough for that to happen. Nope. I was hoping when the killer saw the police swabbing for blood in the tunnel, it would make him or her twitchy enough for me to catch them.

I reached into my pocket and pulled out the notecard. "I also sneaked into Pauley's room and found a postcard wedged behind the desk. It's of the night shift workers. When I flipped the card over, I could make out what looked like either "sh" or "st" on back.

Detective Hackett took the postcard from me and carefully examined it. "Which you take to mean..."

"He believed the killer was either Dr. Stark, Nurse Shue, or Stew Rodgers. I've heard from Mac and a couple others how sharp Pauley was even though he wasn't a cop anymore, and he'd had a stroke. I think Pauley was leaving a clue."

"Makes sense. I didn't work directly with Paul, but his reputation was legendary around here."

I smiled at that. "It was legendary at the nursing home, too. Now, I'm thinking the tunnel could be how the killer is moving around in a time when he's not supposed to be at his job. I was told the only people with keys to all side doors were Dr. Stark and the head nurses. And seeing as how his father worked there, it's totally possible for Dr. Stark to have known about the tunnel."

"It will take time to find a judge to sign off on a search warrant on the assertion that there *might* be blood in a secret tunnel." Detective Hackett narrowed his eyes and pursed his lips. "I will be at Gravestone Manor sometime tonight to speak with Dr. Stark about this new relationship development."

"Good."

"I won't waste my breath and tell you that as a civilian, you really have no business messing with my investigation."

I grinned and stood up. "Good. I'd hate for you to waste your breath."

CHAPTER 15

By the time Nikki dropped me off at the nursing home, I only had forty-five minutes to change into my uniform and clock in. I'd need all forty-five minutes just to wiggle into those dang support hose.

But first I wanted to check on Mac and see how he was doing. I walked up the front stairs of Gravestone Manor and smiled when I saw Billy outside smoking his cigarette.

"Hey." I sat down next to him on the bench. "How's Mac?"

Billy exhaled his smoke before answering. "Doin' good from what I hear."

"Can I ask you a question?"

"Shoot."

"What do you know about this place? Like, do you know anything from when it was a mental hospital?"

"Nah. I'm a little young for that. Probably Nurse Lohman could answer those questions." Billy furrowed his brow. "I think the only thing I really know is that something happened out here and they closed the place down for like almost ten years or something. When I was a teenager, this was the place you'd go on a dare. It's always been rumored to be haunted, but until recently, I didn't believe it."

I stood up. "I'm gonna try and sneak down to see Mac before I clock in."

Billy grinned then puffed on his cigarette. "Good luck with that."

I walked up the last of the steps to the front door and went inside. Nurse Lohman was behind the nurses station, eyeing me suspiciously.

Or maybe that's just how I felt.

"Good afternoon, Lexi," Nurse Lohman said.

"Good afternoon." I walked over to the counter. "Nurse Lohman, did you work here back when this place was a mental hospital?"

Nurse Lohman's already stern face hardened even more. "No. I was a nurse at a Kansas City hospital."

"Did you grow up around here?" I asked.

"Fifteen minutes away in a different suburb of Kansas City."

"So you don't know about the history of Gravestone?"

Nurse Lohman stared at me unblinking for ten seconds. "Do I look like the type of woman who would go in for gossip?"

I almost grinned at that image. But I reminded myself I was a professional—even if my 80s hair said otherwise. "No, ma'am. You do not."

"If you'll excuse me, I need to see to these charts."

I waited until she turned around before sprinting down the hall into the solarium. Isabella and Henry were sitting at one of the tables, so I slowed down and sauntered over to them. So much for sneaking through the tunnel on this floor.

"Hey, guys." I pulled out a chair and sat down. "I only have a few minutes."

"Have you been down to see Mac?" Isabella asked, her eyes brimming with tears.

"I have. In fact, I can't stay long because I'm about to sneak down again before I clock in."

"How's he doing?" Henry asked.

"Pretty good," I said. "He's in good spirits."

"I'm glad to hear that," Isabella said. "We were worried."

I waited for her to continue but she didn't.

"Worried about what?" I asked.

Isabella glanced over at Henry before answering. "Years ago, when he was younger, Mac was a pretty famous jockey and horse trainer."

I shouldn't have been surprised at that. His stature alone made him an excellent choice to ride horses.

"When he got too old to ride professionally, he stepped down and started training horses and riders," Henry said. "He continued to train until about two years ago. One day, one of the horses kicked him in the head. It did something to his brain. Scrambled it. He was in a coma for quite a while. When he finally came out of it, he started telling people he was MacGyver. And he seriously believed it. Still believes it."

Mac had suffered a traumatic brain injury. It made perfect sense now. Knowing about his kick to the head made the puzzle pieces fit together.

"Is he married?" I asked.

"He was," Henry said. "His wife passed away shortly after his accident, which is why I believe he's never fully recovered. He likes the bubble he's in."

"He does have a son who visits regularly with his young wife and new baby," Isabella said.

"Well, I can promise you," I said, "he was the same, adorable Mac we've all come to know and love when I left him this morning."

Isabella sniffed and dabbed at her eyes. "I'm so glad."

"I gotta run," I said. "I'm going to sneak down to see him. I'll update you on his demeanor during dinner tonight."

Isabella laid her wrinkled, cold hand on my arm. "Be careful, dear."

I winked at her. "Always."

With a wave to her and Henry, I jogged back to the main entrance of the building. Nurse Lohman was still going over paperwork, so I scrambled up the stairs as fast as I could. When I reached the second floor, I took an immediate left and jogged down the hallway to the tunnel.

Peeking into the living room and lounge area, I was relieved to see there wasn't anyone there. I figured Nurse Shue and Stew were probably in their rooms getting ready to clock in. I pushed the tunnel door open, sent a light globe up into the air, and headed down the steps. Not wanting to get Mac in trouble if the police found his matches, I slowed at the first floor and bent down to retrieve the match he'd dropped last night.

My heart lurched when I realized it was gone. I frantically searched the floor, thinking maybe I'd accidentally kicked it against the wall when I ran by. But no...the match was nowhere to be found.

That meant Mac and I were definitely not the only ones traveling the tunnel.

I dimmed the light and brought my glitter globe down to within a few inches of my face. I had to be more careful

137

with my magic now that I had undeniable proof that I wasn't the only one taking the tunnel.

I thought about my list of suspects and once again Dr. Stark came to the front of my mind. After all, his dad worked at Gravestone for years. His dad could have known about the tunnel and told him.

Had Stew or Nurse Shue ever dropped hints that they knew about the tunnel? I didn't think so, but it would definitely be in my best interest to find out.

I finished jogging down the stairs and carefully made my way around the small splatter of stain on the ground. If it *was* blood, I didn't want to contaminate the scene any more than I already had. With a flick of my wrist, I popped the globe and plunged myself into darkness.

I didn't bother opening myself up to see if I could sense anyone around. It was too oppressive. I didn't have the ability to combat all the different energies I felt down in the dungeon.

Instead, I slid open the door and took off down the corridor. When I reached the infirmary, I rested my head against the wall and listened to see if I could hear voices inside the room.

Lookin' for me, kid?

I bent down and picked up Rex.

"Hey, how's it going?" I asked.

Mac's alone. Go now. Go now.

Still cupping Rex, I pushed the door open with my mind and stepped inside. Mac was doing a victory dance of sorts in front of his bed. Gently placing Rex in my pocket, I hurried over to him.

138

"What's going on, Mac?"

Mac spun around and grinned. "Supposedly, I'm breaking out of here tonight. Nurse Lohman came down a while ago and said there was no reason for me to stay down here any longer."

"I spoke with the police today, and they're stopping by tonight to talk with Nurse Shue and some of us about what happened to you."

Mac's eyes widened. "Really? That's good then. The police must think there's more to the deaths."

"I think Detective Hackett does. I told him I'd try and get more information for him tonight when he came by."

"Oh! Speaking of that, I did some snooping of my own after they came and took away my lunch tray. And guess what? I found some old filing cabinets."

I perked up at that. "What? You did, where?"

Mac hitched his thumb next door. "Across from Dr. Stark's office. There's some abandoned filing cabinets and old equipment left over from when the asylum was here. Some of the equipment looks like it dates back to the early eighteen hundreds. I didn't go in and look through anything. I didn't want to get caught."

"Thanks, Mac. I'll go take a look."

Mac nodded solemnly. "Be careful."

With a wave, I hurried to the door and stuck my head out to see if the coast was clear...and practically hit my head against Nurse Shue's breast.

"Oh," I said, jerking back inside the room. "I didn't know you were there."

"Obviously," she said in a sarcastic tone. "What are you doing down here? You aren't allowed."

"I didn't realize I couldn't visit on my own time," I said in the same exact tone she'd used. I wasn't going to let her—a murder suspect—intimidate me. I came from a long line of women with grit. The likes of her didn't scare me. Well, okay maybe a little...but I wasn't going to let her see it.

Nurse Shue narrowed her eyes. "You have eight minutes to get dressed and get clocked in."

Crap! So much for looking through the files right now.

"I'll be ready," I said.

I waited until she walked into the infirmary before sprinting up the stairs two at a time. I sent a grin to Nurse Lohman as I took a sharp right past the nurses station and hustled up those steps, digging out my key to unlock the gate.

"What—how—"

I left a stuttering Nurse Lohman in my dust.

Silently thanking the Agency of Paranormal Peculiarities for making me train in cardio on top of martial arts, I slid the key into the lock. Once I'd closed and locked the gate again, I jogged back to my room.

What's going on, Lexi? Gonna be sick!

"Oops. Sorry, Rex. I forgot you were still in my pocket."

Rex not feel good.

I slowed my steps, waved my hand in front of my door, and took the rat out of my pocket. Entering my room, I set the little guy down on the ground. He wobbled...then went belly down on the floor.

"You okay, Rex?" I asked.

140

Rex will be fine. Just...need...a minute.

"A minute is about all I have. Now, keep your eyes closed while I get dressed."

You ain't got nothin' I'd want to see, human.

Sticking my tongue out at the passed-out rat, I tore off my clothes and threw them onto the bed. Picking up a new uniform, I tossed it over my head and smoothed it down my body. I decided to forgo the stupid panty hose.

I picked up my socks and sniffed. No doubt about it...any longer in this time period, and I'd have to wash the socks.

"You coming, Rex?"

Be down...in a while...still need...rest.

Luck was on my side when I crept down the stairs five minutes later. Nurse Shue and Nurse Lohman were going over charts, so they paid me no attention on my descent.

I took a left and headed toward the solarium and recreational room. With it still being a couple hours before dinner, I wasn't sure where everyone would be. I found Nikki talking with Jokester Norman from last night in the rec room. Her eyes widened when she saw me. She turned on the TV for Norman, patted his shoulder, and hurried over to me.

"Oh, gosh! Like, do I have some gossip for you!"

"You spoke to your mom?" I asked.

Nikki nodded excitedly...her mile-high bangs bobbing in the air. "She said she didn't know if it was gospel or not, but what she remembers about the incident out here from nineteen seventy-six was that a psychiatrist was shot and killed. She said she couldn't remember the doctor's name, but, like, oh my gosh! Can you believe that?"

Yes, I can. What I can't believe is that no one knows anything more.

I spent the next hour getting residents ready for dinner and formulating a plan on how to get downstairs to see if there was anything in the filing cabinets Mac found. And wondering when Detective Hackett would make his appearance.

CHAPTER 16

Mac was released and in the rec room by the time dinner rolled around. I was thankful for that. One less worry on my mind.

"Hey, Lexi," Mac said when I walked into the rec room. "You're just in time. I was showing Mrs. Dial here how to fix a blown fuse using one of your gum wrappers."

I watched in astonishment as Mac wrapped the foil around the long tube and explained why it would work.

"Is that safe?" I asked.

It didn't seem safe...at all.

"It will hold until Mrs. Dial can get a new fuse," Mac said. He looked up at me and grinned. "See, I told you there were a lot of useful ways to use gum wrappers."

I shook my head and promised myself when I got back home, I'd YouTube it and see if he was correct.

I came up with a plan to get downstairs in the form of a distraction. But I knew it had to be more than just Rex running around chasing Stew. I was going to need something big...something monumental. Something only Isabella and some of her lady friends could pull off.

I let Isabella in on the plan, gathered up the supplies, and then sat back and waited until six-thirty. Not just because by then dinner would be over, but I knew Isabella would need all that time to explain to the other women what to do.

At exactly six-thirty, once all the trays had been removed and residents were relaxing, Isabella took my cue and the fireworks began.

Isabella hopped up from the small table she was sitting at with Henry and Mac, shuffled over to the middle of the room, and began clapping her hands together. All the ladies in the room stood up, and I turned on the silver boombox sitting on the ledge of the wall. Rod Stewart's "Do Ya Think I'm Sexy?" blared out of the speakers. And all eyes turned to the women in the room.

"Let's get it, girls!" Isabella cried out.

One by one the older ladies started gyrating, whooping, and singing at the top of their lungs. Isabella unbuttoned her green sweater, slid it off her shoulders, twirled it around in the air, and let it fly.

It hit Henry square in the face.

That was all it took.

The men whooped and hollered and struggled to their feet to join in. I was pretty sure I saw a dollar bill fly through the air, but I wasn't sure. This was definitely the distraction I needed.

Isabella crooked her finger at Mac and winked, still twirling and shaking her booty while she sang. "If ya want my body, and ya think I'm sexy..."

I'd have given anything at that moment to have a cell phone on me so I could record and play back when I needed a feel-good moment years from now. This was the most amazing, beautiful, and strangely bizarre spectacle I'd ever witnessed.

And it didn't take long for the party poopers to arrive.

"What's going on in here?" Stew demanded.

"This is what we call having a good time," I hollered over the music. "Blowing off a little steam...getting in some exercise."

"This is *your* doing?" he asked.

I shrugged. "Does it look like it's my doing?"

Stew's face turned red. He spun on his heel and headed straight for Isabella.

Rex to the rescue!

Out of the corner of my eye, I saw Rex leap off a table and fly through the air. He landed on Stew's shoulder. Before Stew could react, Rex grabbed hold of Stew's rat tail and started swinging back and forth.

Yeehaw! Ride 'em, cowboy! Giddyup!

I'd have also given anything at *that* moment for Stew to have heard what Rex was saying. It would have definitely given him a heart attack.

"What is it with this rat?" Stew reached behind his head to bat Rex away. "Get off! That hurts!"

But Rex was hanging on for dear life.

Between Rod Stewart, the women squealing and laughing with pleasure, the men whooping and egging on the women, and now Stew throwing a fit, it didn't take long for Nurse Shue, Dr. Stark, and Nikki to arrive.

And only one out of the three looked amused.

"What is the meaning of this?" Nurse Shue demanded.

Rex dropped to the ground and scurried out the room.

Isabella looked at Nurse Shue and gyrated even more. "Just a couple young girls out having a good time." Isabella held out her arms to Dr. Stark. "You wanna boogie, doctor?"

Dr. Stark's eyes grew wide as saucers. "Um. No. I d-don't think I do. But th-thank you for asking."

"Suit yourself, doc," Isabella yelled over the music. "But you don't know what you're missing!"

"Turn that off this minute!" Nurse Shue yelled at me.

I shrugged, then reached over and turned off the music.

"Aww," Isabella pouted. "Well, girls, I guess we have no choice now but to streak!"

Screams of ecstasy filled the air as one by one the older ladies started to fully undress. A bra flew over my head, a wig was tossed, and I'm pretty sure I saw some dentures sail.

"Get these people back in their rooms, now!" Nurse Shue yelled.

Dr. Stark finally snapped out of his stupefied trance. "Yes, this must stop right now."

I caught Isabella's eye and she gave me a slight nod before turning on her heel and shuffling out of the room as fast as her octogenarian legs could travel. "Catch me if you can!"

"After her!" Nurse Shue snapped at me. "Then come back in here and get these others to their rooms."

I nodded and took off into the solarium after Isabella...or so it looked that way. As I sprinted toward the steps that led to the basement, I could still hear Nurse Shue yelling at everyone to return to their rooms.

"Be careful," Isabella said as I flew past her and all but slid down the stairs to the basement. I sailed by the infirmary, waived my hand in the air to open the door I needed, and came to an abrupt stop outside the room opposite Dr. Stark's. Just like in the other rooms, a tiny

146

window butted up against the ceiling. There was still enough sun outside to penetrate the filthy window and give the room a soft glow of natural light.

There were two smashed filing cabinets with four drawers each near the far wall, an abandoned wooden wheelchair sat in the middle of the room, and another rusted out metal gurney with a broken wheel was pushed against another wall. But by far the creepiest thing in the room was the set of chains and wrist cuffs hanging from a wall. I didn't even want to think about how those had been used.

I rushed over to the set of smashed filing cabinets lying on the floor and whipped my hand back hard. All eight drawers flew open at once.

I gave a startled laugh. I hadn't expected that. Squatting down, I rummaged around to see what was in the first drawer. A daily log of some kind took up a majority of the space. It didn't help me any, but I was glad to see the years were in the vicinity of what I was looking for...nineteen seventy-three to nineteen seventy-five.

I shuffled through the second, third, and fourth drawers of the first filing cabinet with dismal results. I was beginning to get worried about being gone for so long when I leaped over the first smashed cabinet and started in on the second one.

When I got to the third drawer, I let out a squeal of excitement. A clipboard with a black piece of carbon paper still attached sat perched on top. I recognized the crinkly paper from a previous case I'd had during the seventies. The black paper was used as a sort of copy machine. People would write on paper that was three sheets thick. The top white paper being the original, and then underneath was the black carbon paper that would transfer the written or typed material to another paper underneath. The paper underneath could be white, yellow, or pink. Sometimes it was hard to read if the person didn't press down exactly the same throughout, but it worked pretty well.

I carefully picked up the clipboard, lifted the black carbon paper to see what was underneath, and scanned the paper.

And nearly fainted from shock.

The tattered sheet was dated one week before Dr. Melvin Stark was shot and killed in nineteen seventy-six. The paper was from Dr. Stark, addressed to Holloway Mental Hospital, and stated that one Amanda Shue needed immediate transfer to their psychiatric treatment facility. He feared she was imprinting her delusions onto other patients. And that her infatuation with him was reaching dangerous levels.

Oh my gosh...Amanda Shue? Was this a relative of Nurse Sandra Shue? Obviously it had to be. Shue wasn't all that common of a name.

Tearing the white paper off the clipboard, I shoved it in the pocket of my uniform and hurried to the door—my mind reeling from what I'd just learned. Cracking the door open a hair, I peeked out into the hallway. I didn't see anyone.

Figuring a staff member wouldn't dare use the tunnel during working hours, I decided to make a run for it up the tunnel stairs to the first-floor solarium.

I waved my hand in front of the tunnel door and it slid open. Dashing across the hall, I careened into the darkened

148

room. Steeling my nerves, I quietly closed the door, ran my hand up the stone wall for guidance, and hurried as fast as I could up to the first floor, not even bothering with a glitter globe.

I took a deep breath and slid open the hidden door. The solarium was quiet. Actually, the whole east wing was quiet. I stepped out into the courtyard, shut the door, and looked in on the rec room. It was empty.

Obviously Nurse Shue wasn't joking around when she ordered everyone to their rooms like naughty children. Someone was going to have to let these people in on the fact if they wanted the facility to run as an assisted living facility, then they needed to stop treating the residents like they were in prison.

Knowing I was going to get called on the carpet and asked where I'd been, I had no choice but to head over to the west wing. As I entered the hallway to pass the nurses station, Dr. Stark and Nurse Shue caught me.

"Where have you been?" Nurse Shue demanded.

I gestured down the hallway toward the solarium. "I was just making sure everyone was back in their rooms."

"Before that," Nurse Shue snapped. "Stew and I have been looking for you."

"Oh, did you need something?" I asked as innocently as I could.

Nurse Shue frowned. "Nikki is gathering the bedding and clothes for the night in the women's hallway. Please assist her. Stew has the men's hallway covered."

"You bet."

As I headed to help Nikki, I couldn't help but wonder where Detective Hackett was. He should have been here by now.

CHAPTER 17

I didn't want to ask who Amanda Shue was in front of Dr. Stark. Mainly because it would be too hard for me to gauge both of their individual reactions. So now I'd have to find a time to catch Dr. Stark and Nurse Shue alone to ask my questions about the elusive Amanda Shue.

I caught up with Nikki at the end of the women's hallway. She'd just finished stuffing a wad of clothes down into the giant cart when she turned and saw me. Her eyes grew wide and she motioned me over to her, her face splitting into a huge grin.

"Like, that was the craziest thing I've ever seen. Clothes were actually coming off! I've already spoken with Isabella, and she's so happy right now. She can't stop laughing and smiling."

I chuckled at the memory of Isabella stripping and running. Mac was going to be impossible to live with now. There would be no denying his claim that all the ladies fall for him.

"And the other women, like, they are just as wound up. They want to start up a weekly dance night."

"Good for them," I said. "Did everything else go okay?"

"Like, oh my gosh, did you see what happened to Stew? That giant rat came out of nowhere and attacked him again!"

"Yeah, I saw. That was weird, huh?"

I wonder where the little daredevil is now?

"Totally weird," Nikki said. "But also totally funny."

A resident's door opened, and a gray-haired older lady with huge framed glasses, kinky curly hair, and a plump round body grinned out at me. I remembered she'd told me her name was Glenda.

"That was so much fun tonight, dear. I hope we get to do it again soon."

I smiled at her. "Thanks for letting me choose a song from your collection."

It was Glenda who'd saved the day by letting us borrow her tape of Rod Stewart. She said her great-granddaughter had left it the last time she'd stopped by for a visit.

"Did you get your tape back?" I asked.

"I sure did," Glenda said. "Nikki here retrieved it for me. I just wanted you to know I hadn't had that much fun in years."

She stepped back into her room and quietly shut the door. I had the Internet to thank for the distraction tonight. I remembered all the memes I'd seen on social media that talked about being old ladies in nursing homes and all the fun they were going to have. I figured...why not make that a reality tonight? This place was way too stuffy as it was.

"Where did you run off to?" Nikki asked.

I sobered immediately. I knew I couldn't tell her about what I'd found. Nikki was already too involved with my investigation. For that matter, so was Mac. I was used to solving crimes on my own. One of the things imprinted on our brains from the Agency of Paranormal Peculiarities is that we can never tell others who we really are...or *what* we really are.

"I had a bathroom emergency," I lied. "If you want, I'll take the cart down to the laundry room for you."

"Thanks. I'm gonna, like, keep checking in on the ladies."

I grabbed the handle of the cart and pushed it down the hall toward the nurses station. I hoped Nurse Shue would be alone by now so I could ask her some pointed questions.

And luck was on my side. As I pushed the cart down the hallway, I overheard Dr. Stark say he needed to retire to his office and work on paperwork. I waited until he walked downstairs before pushing the cart to the nurses station.

"Nurse Shue," I said, "would you mind if I asked you some questions?"

"About what?"

"About the recent deaths here at the nursing home," I said.

Nurse Shue's face closed off. "There's nothing to discuss. We've unfortunately experienced a bump in the road, but the facility is running efficiently now."

Is it?

"Who's Amanda Shue?" I asked.

Nurse Shue's hands jerked, knocking two files to the floor. "Look what you made me do." She bent down and picked them up, still not meeting my eyes.

"Amanda Shue?" I asked again.

Nurse Shue let out a huff and crossed her arms over her chest. "How did you find out about my sister?"

Sister!

"Purely by accident," I said. "I came across something with her name."

"Here? In this facility? After all this time?"

"Yes," I said. "I didn't know she was your sister, just that she was probably a relative since you shared the same last name."

"Amanda was—*is* my sister."

"Was she a patient here at the hospital when it was a mental facility?" I asked, even though I already knew the answer.

Nurse Shue's jaw clenched and her nostrils flared. "Yes."

When she didn't say anything more, I tried for a different approach. "I guess she's not here anymore. Even if the facility closed twelve years ago, I assume she'd be too young for a retirement center."

"My sister and I are twins. I'm Sandy and she's Mandy."

Whoa, didn't see that coming.

"So obviously not old enough for a nursing home," I joked lamely.

"No."

I counted back in my head. "She must have been young when she was here." I tried to sound sympathetic, but my senses buzzed with the need to know everything. "Didn't the hospital close down in like seventy-six?"

Nurse Shue nodded, and she suddenly looked more relaxed. "Yes. To both questions. Mandy was young when she first arrived at Gravestone Asylum—that's still what everyone called it. But, yes, Mandy was here from nineteen seventy-four to nineteen seventy-six. Until they closed the facility down."

"I'm sorry."

154

Nurse Shue shrugged. "Mandy was always an unstable girl. Even when we were little. She'd do mean things, not only to me, but to the other kids at school. It got to where I was tattling to my parents every day. One night, Mandy snapped, and she came after me with a knife. My parents had no choice but to dump her in here. She was only seventeen years old when she went in. Soon to be eighteen. It was our senior year."

I blinked in surprise. I hadn't realized she'd been *that* young. "Was she with other kids or adults out here?"

"Back then it was all lumped together. Young and old alike."

"So she was here when the unfortunate incident took place, and they had to close the facility down?" I asked.

Nurse Shue's eyes widened. "You *do* know a lot about the previous place."

I couldn't tell if she was irritated or amazed. "I don't know particulars. I grew up not too far from here myself, and I think I remember my mom talking about something terrible happening here once."

A total lie, but Nurse Shue obviously bought it.

She nodded. "It happened twelve years ago. I don't know exactly how it all started. Mandy wasn't completely sure either, but..." Nurse Shue trailed off, looking toward the set of stairs leading down to the basement. "Perhaps this isn't the best place to talk about this."

Oh, it's the perfect time and place.

"I'm sorry," I said. "I didn't mean to upset you."

"You haven't upset me. It's just been a long time since I spoke of the event to anyone."

I propped my elbow against the counter and rested my head on my hand. "I've always been interested in local history. I'd love to hear the story."

Nurse Shue sighed. "Like I said, I don't have all the facts. Mandy refused to speak about it after she was transferred. But from what I've come to learn, a psychiatrist at the mental institution was doing unspeakable things to some of the women."

"What sort of things?" I asked.

Nurse Shue's face twisted in disgust. "He was forcing himself on some of the female patients. It was horrible."

"Mandy told you that?" I asked, once again schooling my face to appear sympathetic. "Did it happen to her?"

Nurse Shue shook her head. "No, of course not. But she did tell me when she found out, she encouraged the women to tell their families, and those family members went to the police."

"Who was the doctor that did the terrible things, do you know?"

Nurse Shue's eyes cut again to the staircase. "I actually do."

"Who?"

Nurse Shue swallowed and tugged on her dress. "His name was Dr. Stark."

I made my mouth drop open in shock. "Like Dr. Stark who's downstairs?"

"Don't be silly," Nurse Shue snapped. "He's much too young." She paused dramatically. "It was his father."

This time I didn't have to play at being surprised. "Isn't it a little strange for a man whose father was accused of

156

horrible crimes to come back to the very same facility, buy it, and work here?"

Nurse Shue shrugged. "I have no idea."

Oh, I think you do.

"What happened to Dr. Stark?" I asked, even though I already knew the answer. "Did he go to jail?"

"No. From what I know, when the police came to arrest Dr. Stark, he went raving mad. He shot at the policeman who came to investigate. The officer had no choice but to shoot and kill Dr. Stark. Tragic really."

"Yes, it is. What happened to your sister Mandy?"

Nurse Shue blinked in surprise. "Oh, well Mandy was transferred to another facility for a few more years. Then she was eventually released."

"Do you get to see Mandy very often?"

Nurse Shue was silent a moment. "Why do you ask?"

I shrugged. "I was just curious."

Nurse Shue sighed and got a faraway look in her eye. "Not as often as I probably should. It's complicated. We have separate lives now. Our parents were unfortunately killed in an automobile accident a few years back, so we really don't have a bond keeping us together. She lives about an hour from here and works in a nursing home, too."

I blinked in surprise. "She's in the medical field? Like an aide?"

"She's a nurse."

I hated to sound naïve about such things, but I didn't know that could happen. "I—um—I didn't realize—"

Nurse Shue glared at me. "You didn't realize what?"

"Well, to be honest, I didn't realize that you could be a nurse after having spent time in a mental institution," I admitted.

"This is the nineteen eighties. Not the dark ages. Mandy passed her nursing classes *and* state examination."

"That's great."

I think.

"Granted," Nurse Shue said, "she can't seem to hold down a job for long."

I wonder why.

I shook my head, trying to work past the insanity of what Nurse Shue just told me.

"Is it weird working with young Dr. Stark, knowing what his dad allegedly did to the patients at your sister's institution?"

"No. Our Dr. Stark is a wonderful doctor in his own right. The sins of his father should not reflect onto him."

Wow. True enough.

"I wonder how our Dr. Stark really feels about being here every day after all that's happened?" I mused.

"I have no idea. We've never discussed it."

I blinked in surprise. "You've never discussed what happened out here in all the time you've worked together?"

"No. It's never come up."

I found that hard to believe.

"What about Nurse Noland? Did she know about Dr. Stark's dad and what happened out here?"

Once again Nurse Shue's eyes hardened. "I have no idea what Nurse Noland knew."

158

"But you guys were best friends from what the residents have told me. Surely you guys talked about how odd it was for Dr. Stark to have bought this place and opened up a nursing home here? Or even discussed why he'd want to buy this place?"

"We did not."

I leaned in conspiratorially. "I heard from a couple of the residents that Nurse Noland and Dr. Stark were having an affair."

Anger flashed in Nurse Shue's eyes. "Absolutely not true. That would be frowned upon since Dr. Stark owns the facility."

I took in everything she'd told me. I felt some parts were true...while other parts were lies. I suddenly wished my friend and fellow time-traveling witch, Felicity Warner, was here. She had the ability to discern when someone was lying. Well, *most* times she could. She was still learning about all her new witchy abilities and how they worked. But with the complexity of my current assignment, I'd take what Felicity could discern.

CHAPTER 18

I pushed off the counter as though to leave. "I guess I better get this laundry down to the machines."

"Yes, you should."

I walked a couple feet then stopped. "Oh, real quick. One more question. Do you know who the policeman was who shot and killed Dr. Stark?"

Nurse Shue hesitated only a second before answering. "Yes. I'm aware of who shot and killed Dr. Stark."

"And who was that?" I asked.

"It was actually a former resident here."

"Here?" I feigned shocked. "Really?"

Nurse Shue nodded her head once. "Yes. His name was Paul Ridgeway. He passed away a few days ago. You never had a chance to meet him. I'm surprised Mac didn't mention it to you."

I gasped. "Pauley? He was the policeman who shot and killed Dr. Stark twelve years ago? Wow. Does *our* Dr. Stark know that?"

Nurse Shue shrugged. "I'm sure he does. But we've never discussed it."

Again, I got the feeling she was telling me the truth...yet not. There was something odd I just couldn't put my finger on.

I heard a squeaky wheel and turned to see Stew heading our way, pushing his own laundry cart. I groaned at the thought of being alone with him in the laundry room. While I'd pretty much ruled him out as the killer, I didn't like him any better.

"Well, I better get these down to laundry," I said.

Shoving the loaded-down cart, I hurried through the solarium and into the rec room. I glanced at the clock and saw it was around eight. The kitchen staff would be gone, which meant I'd be completely alone with Stew.

I started pushing the cart again, thinking about what Nurse Shue had just said about her sister also being a nurse, when up popped Rex from inside the sheets.

Hey there! Miss me?

"There you are," I whispered. "I was actually beginning to wonder where you'd run off to."

Just listening in. What's Rex's next job? I'm ready. I'm ready. They don't call me Rex the Ready for nothing.

"I'm not sure right now. I need to go down to Dr. Stark's office and try and talk with him."

Suddenly, Rex hopped down from the sheets and scurried out the door. A few seconds later, I heard Stew yelling and cursing. Chuckling at the rat's antics, I maneuvered the cart around the furniture and into the side laundry room. There were four washing machines, four dryers, two round tables with a couple chairs, and two vending machines. One dispensing candy...the other dispensing cigarettes. I pushed the cart next to one of the washing machines.

Stew headin' your way! I'm gonna take him down. Yes, I am. Yes, I am.

"Where've you been, little rabbit?" Stew's smarmy voice echoed off the bare walls.

Rolling my eyes in disgust, I whirled around and glared at him. "None of your business, rat boy."

Rage flashed in Stew's eyes, and he pushed his cart away from him and into one of the other washing machines. "I think it's time you and I had a little understanding of how things work around here."

I snorted. "Is that so?"

Stew lunged at me, but I was ready for him. I hopped back and laughed when he clutched air and fell forward, grabbing onto a table so he wouldn't fall.

Before he could right himself, I used my powers and slid the table over three feet. Stew, already unstable, pitched forward and fell to his knees.

Good one, Lexi! Bring him to his knees!

"Is that how things work around here?" I asked in a smug, superior voice.

With a growl, Stew lunged to his feet. And again, I was ready for him. I stepped back and planted my left foot on the ground and lifted my right leg up. In one quick motion, I pivoted my hips, extended my right leg out, and kicked Stew in the gut.

Down he went again.

Again! Again! Make him suffer!

"I'd suggest you stay there," I said. "I know moves that will leave you weeping like a little baby."

Stew struggled to his feet, this time grabbing a chair and hurling it in my general direction. I wasn't sure if he meant to hit me with it or just intimidate me. Either way, it didn't work.

When I snorted, he leaped for me again. This time I jumped on my right leg, lifted my left leg high in the air, and threw a front snap kick straight at Stew's chin.

162

A look of pain and surprise fluttered across his face...before he fell back and crashed onto the chairs. He was out before the chairs slid and dropped his body to the ground.

I glanced over at the table and did a double-take. If I didn't know better, I'd swear Rex was doing the Moonwalk across the table.

You kicked his butt! Whoohoo! Way to go, Lexi!

Knowing Stew would have something Mac would want, I jerked his pant pocket to where I could reach inside. Feeling around, I wrapped my hand around the object and lifted it out.

A matchbook. Mac would love this little gift.

I dropped the matchbook in my front pocket and was about to hurry out of the room when I saw Rex bent over Stew.

"What're you doing?" I asked.

Rex stepped back proudly, and I saw Stew's laced knotted together.

He stands up...he falls down. Rex the Rascal wins again!

I laughed. "Let's go. The kick will probably keep him down for a few minutes, and then after he falls again from the laces, he'll have to spend some time untying them. We should have plenty of time to go ask some questions."

I jogged across the solarium and Rex scurried past me, racing down the hall.

When I reached the nurses station I slowed down and tried not to make eye contact. By the time I made it to the men's hallway, Rex skidded to a stop in the middle of the floor.

Mac's in his room. All alone. All alone.

"Thanks, Rex."

I knocked on Mac's door and he motioned me in.

"Everything okay?" I asked.

Mac shook his head slowly, as if getting the cobwebs out. "Yeah. I'm just really tired is all. That little dance session took a lot out of me."

I laughed. "I'm sure it did. You've had a crazy twenty-four hours. You've been possibly drugged and left for dead. Your body is trying to recuperate. Give it some time."

"So what've you discovered?" Mac asked.

I knew I couldn't tell him everything, or he'd want to help. So I went with the old distraction method. "Look what I got for you."

I dug the matches out of my pocket and handed them to him. His mouth dropped open as he snatched them from me. "I know these matches. These are Stew's. This is a bar in town he likes to go to." He looked up at me in awe. "How'd you do it? Sleight of hand? The ole look-over-there trick? What?"

I grinned and shrugged like it was no big deal. "I actually kicked his butt, stole them from him while he was knocked out, and brought them down here to you."

"You didn't!" Mac exclaimed. "Tell me everything."

So I spent a few precious minutes telling him about my front kick and how I put Stew in his place. Mac laughed so hard, I thought at one point his false teeth might fly out of

164

his mouth. After he was done laughing, though, he turned sober.

"Listen, you watch out for him. He's bad news."

"I will," I promised.

"Now, don't think I didn't notice what you did there. I asked if you found anything important."

I sighed and resigned myself to the fact Mac was going to insist on helping me. "First I want to ask you something. I've gone over and over in my head why Dr. Stark would want to kill you. The only thing I can come up with is because maybe he was afraid you would tell the detectives that he and Nurse Noland were dating. Their dating and ultimate breakup is a decent motive for him killing Nurse Noland. By taking you out, he's covering his butt. But what about Nurse Shue? Do you know of any reason why she would want you dead?"

Mac shrugged his shoulders. "No. Like I said, until all this crazy stuff started happening recently, Nurse Noland, Nurse Shue, Dr. Stark, they were all friendly and got along well. Then suddenly, like a day or two before Nurse Noland died, things changed. But that doesn't have anything to do with me. I don't know why Nurse Shue would want me dead."

"I need to go," I said. "I'm going to see what Dr. Stark has to say about this recent development."

"What recent development?"

"I don't have time to explain right now," I said. "I'll catch you up later."

Mac frowned. "Be careful."

"I will. I'll try and check back in with you before I get off my shift. Are you worried about being in here alone tonight?"

Mac scoffed at my ridiculous question. "I'm pretty resourceful. Now that I know someone is after me, I'll take the necessary precautions."

"I'm sure you will."

I hurried out of the room and down the hallway. Nurse Shue was entering another resident's room and didn't pay me any attention. At the nurses station I took a left and headed down to the basement and Dr. Stark's office.

I lifted my hand and knocked lightly at his door. When I didn't get a response, I knocked a little harder.

"What?" Dr. Stark growled.

I figured that was good enough for an invitation to come in. I pushed open the door and walked inside. Dr. Stark was sitting at his desk, head in his hands, a cup of coffee at his elbow. He looked up and scowled.

"What do you need?" Dr. Stark asked. "What could you possibly do next to make this night any worse?"

I blinked in surprise at his accusation, then remembered the earlier scene in the rec room. "Sorry about that. But I really don't think I'm going to do anything that will top the anniversary of your father's death, do you?"

His head jerked up. "What do you know about my father's death?"

I lifted one shoulder. "Just that he was a psychiatrist back when this place was a mental hospital. And in nineteen seventy-six, something happened that caused him to get shot and killed."

A half-truth.

166

Dr. Stark curled his lip and narrowed his eyes. "My father dedicated ten years of his life to this place. He loved his job and the people here. Then suddenly, things changed. He was distracted, came home late. He wasn't acting like himself."

I didn't say anything, just crept forward slowly so I didn't startle him. I didn't want him to stop talking.

"I tried to ask him about it. He'd only say it was a problem at work. But when I tried to push for more, he clammed up. Then—" his voice broke and he cleared his throat. "Then about a week before he died, a detective came to our house to interview my mom. I was attending the University of Kansas and due back in a few weeks to start the Fall semester. Two days later formal charges were filed against my dad."

"And a couple days after that, he would be shot and killed," I said.

"Yes."

I thought about what he'd said about his dad's demeanor. Easily distracted, coming home late, acting like nothing was wrong.

"Do you believe your father did those awful things he was accused of?" I asked.

"Never!" Dr. Stark spat.

"But you do suspect your father was having an affair."

Dr. Stark jerked back as though I'd smacked him. "No, of course not. Never!"

But I saw it. For one brief second, Dr. Stark hesitated and doubt flickered in his eyes.

And then an awful thought popped into my head. What if Dr. Stark was seeking revenge for his father? Maybe the reason Dr. Stark killed Nurse Noland was because he believed she represented the nurse his dad may have been sleeping with. And then he killed Pauley because he was the man responsible for shooting and killing his father.

"I know it was Pauley Ridgeway who shot and killed your father," I said. "How did you cope with that?"

Dr. Stark frowned. "What? How did I cope with what?"

"With seeing your father's killer every day here at the nursing home?"

Dr. Stark stood up and put his hands on his hips. "Why are you asking me all these questions? Who *are* you?"

I held up my hands and took a step back...hoping to show I meant no harm. "Just a curious person is all."

"Well, not that it's any of your business, but I never blamed Pauley for what he did. He had no choice." Dr. Stark rubbed his hands across his eyes. "The night Pauley shot my dad, my dad was actually trying to kill himself. He'd pulled the gun on himself. When he couldn't do it, he pointed the gun at Pauley and started firing. Pauley had no choice but to shoot back. Over the years, I've kept tabs on Pauley. I was instrumental in getting him placed out here when I bought the building and opened the facility."

I bet you were.

"Well," I said, "it's good to know you didn't hold a grudge against him."

"I think it's time you left. I'm sure Nurse Shue is looking for you."

168

"Of course, doctor. Oh, one more thing. Did you know that Nurse Shue's twin sister, Mandy Shue, was a patient at the mental institution during the same time your dad worked here?"

"What?" He looked completely dumbfounded. "What?"

I nodded. "Yes. Mandy would have been around nineteen when the place closed down, and later she was transferred to a different facility. Nurse Shue just finished telling me about her twin sister, Mandy, who lived here during the time your father was a psychiatrist here."

"I can't believe it," Dr. Stark said. "Although, I always had this feeling she knew more about the old place than she let on." He shrugged. "I guess she didn't want to relive it any more than I did."

"I guess not."

I walked out of the room and closed the door behind me. My mind raced with what I'd found out from Dr. Stark. He didn't believe the allegations against his father, but he *did* suspect his father may have had an affair. He also knew Pauley shot and killed his father, but he claimed he didn't blame Pauley, and was in fact on friendly terms with him.

But what bothered me the most was Mac. Where did Mac fit into all this? Why try and kill Mac? If I believed Nurse Shue was the killer, I'd say she killed Nurse Noland out of jealousy. She wanted Nurse Noland's job of head nurse. That was plausible. But I had no real motive as to why she would kill Pauley. Or really even her motive for trying to kill Mac.

On the other hand, both Dr. Stark and Stew had better motives to kill.

Stew wanted Nurse Noland dead because she was on the verge of firing him. He needed this job. It was a weak but plausible motive. I had no motive for him killing Pauley, but I did overhear Stew threaten to kill Mac.

Then there was Dr. Stark. His motive for killing Nurse Noland was stronger. It's the twelve-year anniversary of his father's tragic death. Maybe he snapped...or maybe he had something like this planned all along once he got Pauley transferred here.

He believed Nurse Noland represented the embodiment for his life falling apart. She's the "other woman" in his otherwise perfect childhood. He and Nurse Noland start dating, he makes up some story about her cheating on him—like his father cheated on his mother—and he killed Nurse Noland out of rage and anger.

The motive for Dr. Stark killing Pauley was much easier...Pauley was responsible for shooting and killing his father. And the motive for killing Mac? Mac knew about Dr. Stark and Nurse Noland. He'd caught them kissing. Dr. Stark made Mac promise not to tell anyone. Dr. Stark could just be cleaning house on who might be able to finger him as the killer.

Unfortunately, everything I had was circumstantial. I had nothing concrete. But when I put all the facts together, I couldn't help but lean toward Dr. Stark as the killer. Now I just had to figure out a way to prove it...before he caught on to what I was doing and decided to put me on his list.

CHAPTER 19

I decided to take the tunnel back upstairs so I didn't have to pass the nurses station. I conjured up a glitter globe for minimal light and once again carefully sidestepped the possible blood splatter Detective Hackett was supposed to come extract. When I got to the first floor, I let the purple glitter globe fizzle and fade.

I pulled the door open and was surprised to see Stew sitting at one of the metal tables in the solarium. His head was resting on the table. When I realized he wasn't paying me any attention, I silently slid out and closed the door. I'd just started to tiptoe toward the nurses station when Nikki came walking down the hall.

"There you are," Nikki said. "I was about to take my last ten minute break." She looked at her Swatch watch. "I go home in, like, thirty minutes."

"Let's sit," I said.

Nikki came to a sudden halt when she noticed Stew. "What's up with him? I saw him get an ice pack out of the kitchen. He has a bruise on his chin and cheek."

I repeated what'd happened, and I have to say, I felt pretty badass. Nikki couldn't stop gawking at me with awestruck eyes. It made me feel good. Usually when I spar with my best friends, Vee and Nuala, I can't hold a candle to them. In fact, compared to the other witches I work with at the Agency of Paranormal Peculiarities, I often feel pretty inferior. So to have Nikki look at me like I could single-handedly whip any bad guy...it made me feel invincible.

A commotion at the nurses station caused us both to turn around and see what was going on. My eyes widened when I saw Detective Hackett and Detective Seaver. Detective Hackett pointed a finger at Nurse Shue and scowled.

"Let's see what's going on," I said.

We made our way down the hall and close enough to the counter where we could hear but not be caught eavesdropping. I heard Detective Hackett ask for Dr. Stark. Nurse Shue informed the detective he was in his office.

"What're you two doing standing here?" Stew's voice sounded behind us and Nikki and I both jumped.

That caused Nurse Shue, Detective Hackett, and Detective Seaver to all glance over at us.

So much for hiding.

Nurse Shue narrowed her eyes at us. "Surely you three have more important things to do than stand around here."

"Yes, ma'am," Nikki said.

But she wasn't looking at Nurse Shue when she responded...instead she only had eyes for Detective Seaver.

"Detective Seaver and I know the way to Dr. Stark's office," Detective Hackett said. "We can show ourselves down."

Nurse Shue pursed her lips in anger. "I don't think—"

But she didn't finish her sentence. Instead, everyone turned and stared at the sights and sounds coming from the women's hallway.

Jokester Norman was in a wheelchair he didn't need, pushing himself with his feet, a bottle of Mad Dog 20/20 clutched in his hand. He lifted his bottle in the air when he saw us all standing open-mouthed at the nurses station.

"Hey!" Norman shouted, "It's our detectives from the other day. Don't worry, we aren't exactly drinkin' and drivin' here."

The Beastie Boys' "You Gotta Fight for Your Right" blared out of Isabella's room as the door opened and Mac and Henry came staggering out. Henry's stained, wife-beater undershirt was tucked into khaki pants pulled up to his chest, and he had his arms around Mac's neck...both men singing along to the lyrics.

"What kind of a place are you running here?" Detective Hackett asked Nurse Shue.

"The kind of place I hope I live someday," I said.

Kudos to Mac and the gang for having a good time while they could. I only hoped I could be that fortunate in my nursing home days...dirty dancing and drinking booze. I thought about my fellow cold-case solving witch friends from the Academy of Paranormal Peculiarities and got a little more excited about the decades to come.

Nurse Shue's pinched face turned nearly purple as she looked from Stew to me to Nikki. Something told me we were gonna get a butt chewing when the police left.

"Get those people back into their rooms," Nurse Shue said tightly. "Now."

Stew, Nikki, and I scrambled past the detectives and down the hall toward Isabella's room. Stew broke off and veered left at the men's hallway. Nikki and I continued on until we reached Isabella's room. To our surprise, no one else was in her room. It was just her, rocking out to the Beastie Boys.

When she saw us she turned down the radio. "I saw the police coming down the drive, so I hurried and got Mac. He came up with the plan."

I laughed. "Where'd you get the Mad Dog 20/20?"

Isabella put her finger to her lips. "Shh. I'll never tell."

"I hope Nurse Shue doesn't, like, seriously blow a gasket over this," Nikki said. "She looked really pissed."

"I think Nurse Shue and Dr. Stark have enough on their plates dealing with the police," I said. "But I do need to speak to Detective Hackett."

"Do you need another distraction?" Isabella asked.

I heard the hopeful tone in her voice and knew I'd created a monster.

"No. I think Nikki and I can handle this on our own."

"If you're sure," Isabella said, sounding like her best friend had died.

"How?" Nikki asked. "Like, Nurse Shue is probably at the desk. You won't be able to sneak down."

I forgot Nikki didn't know about the tunnel.

Isabella waved off our offers to help her get ready for bed, saying we were needed in more urgent matters. I knew when this assignment was up, I'd seriously need some time to myself to get over all the emotional baggage. I'd honestly come to care about these old people in the home. They were fun, spontaneous, funny, helpful, nice. And I would miss them when I left. Especially knowing when I got back to my own time, they would all be gone.

174

Twice a year, the Agency made all of the time-traveling witches go through an extensive debriefing. Usually it was held in exotic locations and it was fun and relaxing to brag to the other witches what we'd done on our assignment. But something told me this debriefing would be different. This case would be difficult to talk about without getting emotional about all the people I'd encountered.

Nurse Shue was indeed behind the counter when Nikki and I strolled by. We mumbled something about getting the laundry out of the laundry room and kept on speed-walking. When we got in the solarium, I told Nikki I'd be back in a second, and without further ado, I bolted to the tunnel.

I looked over my shoulder when I entered the tunnel and saw Nikki's mouth drop open. With a grin, I sent her a wave and disappeared into the darkened tunnel.

I flicked my wrist and brought up a soft, yellow glitter globe as I hurried down the steps, careful not to make any noise. With a wave of my hand, I diminished the light as I opened the door. I could hear voices in Dr. Stark's office, so I silently crept to the open door.

"Whoever told you Mac was drugged is mistaken," Dr. Stark insisted. "He takes a nightly sleeping pill. He probably had a bad dream and simply fell out of bed. He was found on the floor in his room."

"So you've told me two times already," Detective Hackett said in a dry tone.

"Look," Dr. Stark said, "I have no idea why all this is happening. I really don't. I'm beginning to think the rumors of curses are true. There's no other explanation."

"There actually *is* another explanation," Detective Hackett said mildly. "And that is that someone in this nursing home murdered Nurse Noland and Pauley Ridgeway in cold blood."

"Impossible!" Dr. Stark exclaimed.

"We'll see," Detective Hackett said. "Thank you for your time, doctor. We can see ourselves out."

I hurried down the hallway toward the infirmary. I wanted privacy when I spoke to Detective Hackett and Detective Seaver. I didn't have to wait long before both men stepped out from Dr. Stark's office. I motioned for them from inside the infirmary.

"Real quick," I said when both men entered the room. "I want to let you know what I found out this afternoon since we spoke."

"And I'll tell you what's coming down the pike," Detective Hackett said.

I filled them in on Nurse Shue's twin sister, Amanda, living at the mental health facility during Dr. Melvin Stark's time, how she was instrumental in having the women come forward with their allegations, and how Mandy Shue was now a nurse in a small town somewhere. I dug in my pocket and pulled out the carbon copied paper I'd found in the abandoned filing cabinets.

Detective Hackett whistled. "Now that's a little weird. I'll see if I can't find out anything more on her. It sounds like Dr. Stark may have been a little afraid of her...or maybe that's how he wanted it to sound. Maybe this Mandy Shue knew what was going on and he was trying to send her away before things got too far out of control."

176

There was a lot in that statement. Too much for me to try and think about right now.

"Also, Dr. Stark admitted to me that he believes his father was having an affair with one of the nurses," I said. "I have to wonder if maybe that isn't a motive for him to kill Nurse Noland. Like he saw her as the replacement for his mom or something like that."

"I like it," Detective Hackett said. "You should know, the reason it took me so long to get here is because I had to track down a prosecuting attorney and explain about the possible blood. He said he'd try and get ahold of a judge tonight to get us a search warrant. It took hours just to get that done."

"So maybe by tomorrow you'll be able to get the warrant?"

"I'm counting on it," Detective Hackett said.

We parted ways, the two detectives leaving up the steps, and me going back through the tunnel. By the time I got upstairs, Nikki was getting ready to go for the night. I asked her if she could pick me up around eleven the next day so we could head to the police station to see if there was any new developments.

"I'll be here," she promised.

I spent the next hour checking on residents who couldn't sleep...or who wouldn't sleep. Namely, Mac.

"I know what I have to do," Mac said. "Stay up all night. I didn't take my sleeping pill. No one is going to get the jump on me again."

"I'm not sure that's a good idea," I said.

"It's all I got," Mac said.

I sighed and thought about what I could do. I knew there was no way I could stay up all night in his room to watch over him, so I did the next best thing. "Mac, do you trust me?"

"I do," Mac said without hesitation.

"If I tell you I can guarantee your safety tonight, would you go to bed then?"

Mac narrowed his eyes. "You can guarantee my safety?"

"I can."

Mac shrugged as though it was no big deal. "Sure."

I let out a small laugh. "Well, that was easy."

Mac gave me a searching look. "If you say you can protect me, then I believe you. I'll go to bed."

I left his room and went in search of Rex.

I sat down at a table in the solarium, cleared my mind, and took a few deep breaths. "Rex? Where are you?"

Right here! Right here! Whatcha need, Lexi?"

I opened my eyes and smiled down at the rat as he scrambled to climb up the leg of a chair.

"Hey, Rex. I need you to keep watch over Mac tonight. Can you do that for me?"

You bet! You bet! They don't call me Rex the Guardian for nothing.

Rex scurried off to go see after Mac, and I breathed a sigh of relief. One thing I could cross off the list for tonight. Not that I really expected Nurse Shue or Dr. Stark to try and knock off Mac within the next two hours of our shift, but I did give my word.

I wandered into the laundry room and decided to fold the laundry. Usually the graveyard shift took over the

178

laundry, but I really just wanted to stay out of Stew and Nurse Shue's way.

Once the laundry was folded, I crossed over to the window in the rec room to see if Dr. Stark was still around. It was ten-thirty. I caught sight of him walking to his Jeep and couldn't help but notice he was running a little late tonight.

I watched him pull out of the parking lot. While I had a hard time picturing him somehow luring Nurse Noland to the stairs and then pushing her down them, and then doing something to Pauley so it looked like he had a stroke and fell down...I couldn't rule out he was my number one suspect.

"Whaddya starin' at?" Stew asked.

I turned around. "Nothing."

"Did you bring the police here tonight?" Stew asked.

"No," I lied.

"Well someone did," he sneered, "and it wasn't me."

I shrugged and went to walk around him. He stepped sideways to block me.

"Do you really think that's smart?" I asked. "Or have you already forgotten why it is you're sporting a nice bruise on your face?"

Stew scowled. "You won't always be on guard."

I snorted. "I'm fairly certain I can take you with one hand behind my back."

I pushed past him and marched out of the rec room. I had a sudden desire to shower and wash everything about this place off my body.

CHAPTER 20

I woke up late the next morning stiff and sore. I'd tossed and turned most of the night thinking about all the facts I knew. I wasn't sure what time it was when I finally did sleep, but it was definitely early morning hours.

If it was the last thing I did, I would capture the killer tonight. No way could I spend one more day on the miserable mattress. I missed my Posturepedic adjustable bed.

I went to the mirror and was relieved to see my hair wasn't as poofy as it had been yesterday. I didn't dare wash it because I had no idea how to style it. Pulling out the miniature can of hairspray, I pulled my bangs straight up off my head and sprayed them. I seriously had doubts that this was what the hairspray would be used for, but desperate times called for desperate measures. I made sure not to use too much.

I decided to see if I could scrounge up some food from the kitchen down the hall. I was practically to the living room and kitchen area when I finally saw the yellow tape in front of the secret passageway. The tape ran from edge to edge of where the door would be, making it look to the casual observer that a huge "X" had been stuck to the wall. Before I could inspect closer, I heard voices coming from the kitchen and realized with dread that it was Nurse Shue and Stew.

"Good morning." I put a fake smile on my face and sauntered over to where they were. "I haven't had time to go into town yet to get groceries. I thought maybe there might be something down here I could eat."

Nurse Shue hesitated a fraction of a second. "There are scrambled eggs in the skillet. I just made them."

Stew shoved toast in his mouth but said nothing. The bruise on his chin moved with each bite he took.

"I'm pouring some coffee," Nurse Shue said. "Would anyone like some?"

"I would," Stew said.

"Not me." I'd learned the hard way that the coffee I was used to wasn't the coffee of decades past.

Nurse Shue turned and busied herself over by the white plastic coffee pot. Like that wasn't a toxic poisoning waiting to happen.

I scraped the last of the scrambled eggs onto a paper plate, grabbed a fork out of a drawer, and dug in. I'd been able to sneak a couple rolls out of the kitchen last night, but I hadn't had anything decent to eat in a while.

A few minutes later Nurse Shue set a cup of coffee down in front of Stew.

"As I was telling Stew just now, Detective Hackett and three police officers arrived at eight o'clock this morning with a search warrant."

I made my eyes go wide, hoping for a shocked innocent look. "Really? Does it have something to do with the tape I just saw on the wall?"

Nurse Shue gave a hurt nod. "It seems there's a secret passage in the nursing home that no one ever knew about."

Oh, someone knows.

"I can't believe that," Stew said. "Right there on our floor the whole time. Now I want to explore."

"I wouldn't," I said. "That's why the tape's up. So you don't go exploring."

Stew scowled. "I'm aware of why the tape is there."

I shrugged indifferently, knowing it would piss him off. "Just making sure."

"Anyway," Nurse Shue continued, "somehow the police learned about the passageway and someone informed them there may be blood in the tunnel."

"Whoa," Stew said. "This is insane. How would the police find out about it?"

Nurse Shue looked at me. "I'm not sure. But I have my suspicions."

"Don't look at me," I said. "I just started working here two days ago!"

"Be that as it may," Nurse Shue said, "the tunnel runs between the basement all the way up to the second floor here. I haven't been downstairs to see, but I did speak to Detective Hackett this morning and he said there's tape on the first floor in the solarium where another tunnel door is, as well as where it emptied out at in the basement."

"I never saw a door in the solarium," Stew said.

I wisely kept my mouth shut.

"Lexi," Nurse Shue said, "could you clean the pan, please."

"You bet," I said. "Thanks again for the eggs."

Nurse Shue nodded.

"Yeah, thanks for getting me coffee," Stew said.

He took another big swallow, his eyes never leaving mine.

182

"I will see you both at precisely three o'clock downstairs," Nurse Shue said.

She walked out without a backward glance. Stew cleared his throat, grabbed his mug of coffee, got up from the table, gave me another hateful glare, and walked out, too. Leaving me alone.

I wolfed down the rest of my eggs, cleaned the kitchen, and still had time on my hands before Nikki came to pick me up. Walking back down the hallway to my room, I couldn't help but wonder what all Detective Hackett had found. Was it really blood in the tunnel? And, if so, who did it belong to? And had Nurse Shue known about the tunnel? I couldn't tell by her reaction.

Morning, Lexi!

"Hey, Rex." I opened my bedroom door and sat down on the bed. "How did Mac sleep?"

Like a baby!

"I'm going into town to see what the police know. Keep a watch out for me?"

You got it!

At precisely eleven o'clock, Nikki's Pinto came chugging up the long driveway. She parked in the circular drive, and I ran down to meet her. I decided to wear my uniform just in case we ran a little late.

"Thanks for picking me up today," I said. "Guess what? They already came with a search warrant. I'm anxious to know if Detective Hackett heard back from anyone yet."

"This is, like, getting totally insane."

By the time we pulled into the police station and made our way inside, it was almost eleven-thirty. The lady behind the desk greeted us as though we were expected.

Detective Hackett ushered us back to his office and motioned for us to have a seat. Before he could begin, Detective Seaver opened the door and ambled in.

"I was wondering if you needed Nikki," the young detective said, "or if she was free to come with me?"

Detective Hackett waved his hand through the air. "She's free to go if she wants."

"See ya," Nikki said as she grabbed her Jordache purse and followed Detective Seaver out the room.

"I'm assuming you've heard by now that we served the search warrant to extract the possible blood splatter from the tunnel?"

I nodded. "Nurse Shue was in the upstairs kitchen this morning, and she told Stew and me about it."

"We had to ask Dr. Stark to move out of his office so he didn't get in the way," Detective Hackett said. "He seemed genuinely surprised at the location of the hidden tunnel. He claimed he had no idea."

"Yeah, Nurse Shue and Stew pretty much said the same thing," I said.

"When the lab guys sprayed luminol on the stairs and floor, you could see traces of blood."

I sucked in a breath. "So I was right? It was blood?"

Detective Hackett snorted. "Why am I not surprised I don't have to explain what luminol is? But, yes, it looks like there was blood in the tunnel."

"Wow. So hopefully you can figure out who the blood belonged to."

He nodded. "I also spoke to Nurse Shue this morning about her sister. Did she not tell you?"

I thought back to what Nurse Shue had said. "I guess maybe she did mention you told her about the tape that was put up on the first floor and basement."

"I wanted to see her reaction when I asked her about the tunnel. I also questioned her about her sister."

I groaned. "No wonder she thinks I'm the one that told you about the tunnel. I asked her about her sister last night."

"Well, I asked her where her sister was currently working, and she told me. I have a call into the nursing home to see what I can find out about Mandy Shue."

"You don't think this Mandy has anything to do with Nurse Noland's death or the death of Pauley, do you?"

"No. But I have to rule out everything," Detective Hackett said. "I'm getting down to the end of the wire, and I still just have circumstantial evidence. I need something big to tie these two deaths together or I'm afraid once again I'll be pressured to close this case."

***

Nikki parked her Pinto around back of Gravestone Manor in the employee parking lot. We had five minutes before we were due to clock in. I was glad I'd worn my uniform. Again, sans those gawd-awful control top hose.

After leaving the police station, Nikki had taken me to a convenience store where we filled up on Tab and Reese's

Pieces. If I wasn't careful, I was going to go back to my time five pounds heavier.

"There you two are," Nurse Shue said as we walked to the nurses station to get our daily assignments. "Lexi, I want you to take the men's hall and see if anyone needs anything."

"Sure." I looked down the hallway into the solarium but didn't see Stew. "Is Stew not here?"

Nurse Shue shook her head. "He isn't feeling well. I made him some tea and told him to go sit in the rec room and drink it. Hopefully he'll feel better shortly. So I need you to fill in for him until he gets back on his feet."

I nodded. "You got it."

Nikki and I parted ways at the split in the hall. I took a left and started popping into the rooms to see who needed help before dinner.

"So what's the plan for tonight?" Mac asked as I smoothed out the wrinkles in his bed.

Yeah, what's the plan for tonight? We gonna rumble? They don't call me Rex the Rumbler for nothing!

I glanced down by the bed post and bit the inside of my mouth to keep from laughing. Rex was standing on his hind legs and punching the air with his front paws. I was definitely gonna miss him.

"I'm going to put more pressure on Dr. Stark. I need to break him. I don't have time to wait around on the coroner to give his opinion, and I certainly don't have time to wait for the lab results to come back regarding the blood in the tunnel. I need to do this now."

Mac cocked his head at me. "Are you leaving us?"

186

"What? No. I mean—no. I just need to get this settled. Aren't you ready to have answers?"

"I am. If you need help tonight, you let me know."

"I will," I said. "You're my go-to guy, Mac."

By the time I finished making sure everyone was taken care of and ready for dinner, my stomach was in knots. Stew still wasn't feeling better, so Nurse Shue gave him one more round of cold medicine and hot tea, then told him to call it a night and go upstairs to rest if he still wasn't feeling well.

I caught sight of Dr. Stark in the solarium and jogged over to greet him. This would be the perfect opportunity to ask him about the tunnel.

"Dr. Stark, can I ask you a question?"

He looked at me warily. "Yes?"

"It's not really a big deal. I just noticed the tape up on the walls, and I was told it was a secret doorway of some kind. Did you know about it?"

"No. It was a complete surprise to me when the police showed up with a warrant this morning."

He turned and strode out of the solarium, leaving me to wonder if he was lying or telling the truth. Could it be he really didn't know about the tunnel?

I think Stew's about to kick the bucket.

I looked down at Rex. "What?"

He looks like death. Very sick! Very sick!

At seven o' clock, right in the middle of helping residents back to their rooms to get ready for bed or watch TV in the privacy of their rooms, Detective Hackett, Detective Seaver, and two other police officers barged into Gravestone Manor and demanded to see Dr. Stark.

Nikki and I huddled together in between the doorway of the women's hallway and nurses station and listened to Detective Hackett ask Dr. Stark to accompany him to the police station to answer some questions. He assured Dr. Stark he wasn't under arrest, but a few more questions had come up that needed to be addressed. A few seconds later, they led a stunned Dr. Stark out the door.

Nikki said. "What's going on? Why did they take Dr. Stark?"

Nurse Shue shook her head. "I don't know. All Detective Hackett said was he wanted to question Dr. Stark more about the recent deaths of Nurse Noland and Paul Ridgeway."

I furrowed my brow. Was this just a ruse to try and get a confession from Dr. Stark? As far as I knew, nothing new had come to light in the case.

"I'm not feeling well," Stew said. "I'm going upstairs."

For the first time that evening I really looked at Stew. Rex was right, he didn't look well. He was pale, sweating, and if the way he was holding his stomach was any indication, I'd say he was having major stomach problems.

"Go," Nurse Shue said. "Here." She thrust another cup at him and waved him off upstairs. "You two need to finish checking on the residents. We are down an aide, so each of you take a wing and go."

I took a left and headed down the men's hallway.

I told ya he looks bad.

"Keep an eye on him," I said. "I don't think you can fake symptoms like that, but just in case."

On it!

188

Rex took off down the hall toward the nurses station, being sure to hug the wall as much as possible. It wouldn't do for him to get caught by Nurse Shue.

By the time I finished working the men's hall, it was almost nine o'clock. I was hungry and ready for a break. I headed toward the rec room to see if the cooks had left anything out.

"Hey, Lexi."

I smiled at Nikki who was straightening up the recreational room.

"I'm starving," I said. "I'm gonna go see what the cooks left."

I rummaged around in the kitchen and came out a few minutes later with a roll and leftover turkey. It was the driest sandwich I'd had in a long time, but I didn't care.

"Are you going to be okay when I leave at nine?" Nikki asked.

"Whaddya mean?" I asked.

"I just hate leaving you alone here with only Nurse Shue. Dr. Stark is gone, and Stew is upstairs sick. It will only be you and Nurse Shue."

I stopped chewing and thought about that. Was it on purpose? Had Nurse Shue somehow planned that? No. I couldn't come up with a plausible scenario how she could have done that. It was just pure unfortunate luck on my part.

"It'll be okay. I'll stay out of her way. Maybe go hang with Isabella and Mac until my shift is done at midnight."

I helped Nikki finish straightening the rec room, then said goodnight as she clocked out and headed home.

CHAPTER 21

By the time ten o'clock rolled around, I was bored out of my mind. I didn't even have Stew to pick on. I decided to see if Isabella was still awake and quietly slipped down the hallway to her room.

"Who is it?" she called.

"It's me, Lexi."

The door swung open. "Oh, Lexi. C'mon in."

Something was off. I closed my eyes and felt a male presence. "Come out, Mac."

He popped up from beside the bed. "How did you know?"

I chuckled. "Lucky guess. You better not get caught in here, or Nurse Shue will have your hide."

"I was just changing a lightbulb for Isabella," Mac said. "No biggie."

"Uh huh. Listen, I need—"

I was cut off by a knock at the door. Before any of us could react, Nurse Shue opened the door. When she caught sight of Mac, her lips pinched together.

"Why am I not surprised at this?" she demanded.

"It's not what you think," Mac said. "Isabella's light burned out and I was changing the bulb for her."

"Get out," Nurse Shue said. "You know you aren't supposed to be in here after seven."

"Rules, rules, rules," Mac grumbled. "It's like we're teenagers again."

190

I laughed. I couldn't help it. He was right. So what if he wanted to hang out with Isabella for a while? The man was in his eighties. He deserved that right.

Nurse Shue's eyes cut to me. "I need to speak to you both, now."

Mac sighed and headed toward the door. Nurse Shue stepped back to let him pass. I followed close behind. Mac and I were standing outside the door when Isabella sneezed four times in a row.

"Bless you," I said. "Bless you. Bless you. Bless you."

And just like that...it clicked into place.

I jerked my head over to Nurse Shue. But before I could react, she shut the door to Isabella's room, pulled out a syringe, and pressed it to Mac's neck.

"Don't make any sudden move," Nurse Shue said. "I have enough paralytic in this syringe to take down a rhino."

Mac's eyes were wide, and I could see he was trying to put the pieces together. I needed to come up with a plan, so I tried to stall.

"Pauley wasn't cursing people," I said. "He was trying to tell them it was you. Wasn't he? He wasn't saying, 'curse you,' he was saying, 'Nurse Shue.' Only he wasn't able to produce the words correctly."

"It was only a matter of time before someone would figure it out, though," Nurse Shue said. "So I went to his room right before shift change with a syringe full of air. He was dozing in his chair and didn't see it coming until it was too late. I plunged it into the base of his neck. Then I waited. When he started to show signs of having a stroke, I stood him up and pushed him over. He hit his head, and that was it."

I thought back to that night and to what Judy had told me. "Did you do something to the laundry room?"

Nurse Shue chuckled. "I played up the curse. I knew that aide's routine because Nurse Wilson would leave a list of things for her to do on the desk, and it was always the same. I sneaked down using the tunnel and hid in the laundry room closet. After she put in the load of clothes and left, I tipped over the carts and wrote on the table. Scared her to death!"

"So now what?" I asked. "You can't seriously think to kill both me and Mac and get away with it?"

"Now the three of us are going to go for a little walk," Nurse Shue said.

"Why not let Mac go and just take me?" I asked.

To his credit, Mac hadn't said one word or moved one inch since my discussion with Nurse Shue.

Nurse Shue scoffed. "Because, he just stood right here and listened to me spill the whole story. Now, Lexi, you need to slowly walk toward the steps by the front door. We're all gonna take a little trip down them." She giggled at her statement.

"I can't believe you killed Pauley," Mac said. "He was a great guy."

"He shot and killed Dr. Stark." Nurse Shue pushed Mac forward enough to propel me back toward the nurses station. When we passed the set of stairs that led up to the second floor, I looked up them and thought about screaming for Stew and the other aide who lived up there.

192

Nurse Shue must have seen the look on my face because she snorted. "Don't even bother. I've taken care of Stew. He's so sick he wouldn't be able to help you even if he wanted. And that other guy up there is like a vampire. He never leaves his room or goes outside."

"What did you do to Stew?" I asked, trying to distract her while I figured out a plan to get Mac and me out of the mess we were in.

"Gave him about four doses of antifreeze. Once in his morning coffee. Another three doses throughout the night. He's done."

"Why?" I asked. "What's going on?"

And why the hell don't they have cell phones in this time for me to call for help!

We were all three at the top of the stairs that led to the basement. The same set of fifteen stone steps that Nurse Noland had supposedly fallen down. Mac was just a fraction of a hair closer to the steps than I was, with Nurse Shue directly behind him holding the syringe to his neck.

"Which one of you will I push down the stairs first?" Nurse Shue mused. "Mac. You die first. You die first because you violated my sanctuary. You've been running around in the secret tunnel. You've been a very naughty boy."

Without warning, she plunged the needle the rest of the way into Mac's neck. But before she could push down on the plunger and empty the syringe, I ran straight into her, knocking her off balance.

Unfortunately, the momentum also knocked Mac down. I watched in horror as he pitched against the side of the wall before sliding down and rolling sideways down the steps. I was so shocked I couldn't even scream.

I took off after him, but only made it halfway down the stairs before Nurse Shue grabbed me by my hair and yanked me back.

I cursed and tried to kick my leg back to nail her wherever I could. I was still facing forward and relieved to see Mac groan and try to sit up.

"Stop kicking," Nurse Shue demanded.

But I wasn't about to stop. I lifted my leg back again to kick her.

"Have it your way," Nurse Shue said in my ear. It wasn't until I was nearing the bottom of the stairs that I realized what she'd done. She'd used her foot and kicked me down the rest of the stairs. Unable to stop my momentum, I landed on my knees and slid into Mac.

Pain radiated throughout my body, and for a few seconds my vision blurred. I was about to try and help Mac to his feet when Nurse Shue grabbed me by my hair again. This time a syringe was pressed against my neck.

"If I couldn't get Mac, I'll get you with the drug," she said.

Think! Think!

Did you say Rex the Rat to the rescue?

I nearly wept with joy when I saw Rex fly through the air off the wall and leap onto Nurse Shue's face. Or at least that was the plan until Nurse Shue loosened her hold on me, reached up and grabbed Rex out of the air, and pitched him against the wall. His little body hit with a deafening thud, and I heard him whimper in pain.

194

"You bitch!" I screamed as I lowered my head and ran into her gut. We both fell back onto the tarp that was blocking off the west wing. I heard the syringe drop, but didn't see where it landed. I struggled to get my footing but slid off the slick plastic. Nurse Shue grabbed hold of my hair, and I went in for the kill shot. Gathering electrical momentum in my fists, I punched her as hard as I could in the chest. Not that I really thought I could stop her heart...but it was worth a shot.

It was a hard enough hit she had to gasp for air, and I took that reprieve to scoop up Rex and gently lay him in my pocket. Bending down, I lifted Mac up by his arms and had him loop his left arm over my shoulder. I started down the long hallway, hoping to escape through the secret tunnel. Crime tape up or not...I didn't care.

"Where do you think you two are going?" Nurse Shue demanded.

I looked over my shoulder and groaned. She was gaining on us. If I were alone, I'd have no problem going hand to hand with her. But I couldn't leave Mac behind. And I couldn't risk him seeing me use magic.

"Leave me," Mac whispered. "You need to go. You can outrun her through the tunnel."

I looked down into his old, wrinkled face and my eyes filled with tears. There was no way I could leave him at the hands of Nurse Shue so I could escape. In her rage, she'd take it out on Mac. And he was in no shape to fend her off. I could tell a little of the paralytic drug had entered his body. His movements were sloppy and he was starting to drool.

I had no choice. Hitching him up against my side, I pushed on. I was about to wave my hand and push open the tunnel door—even though it meant exposing my magic. But I didn't care. My handlers could come in and worry about wiping away any traces of Nurse Shue or Mac seeing me use magic. They'd hate it, but if it meant saving Mac and me...I'd do it.

"Give me your hairspray," Mac whispered.

"What?"

"Your hairspray you carry around," he said. "Give it to me."

I stopped and reached into my pocket, careful not to disturb Rex, and thrust it at Mac. At the same time I pivoted and kicked out at Nurse Shue. I caught her right above the knee. She screamed in pain and went down, clutching her knee.

"Watch this," Mac said. "Another useful way to use hairspray."

He fumbled inside his pocket and took out one of his matches. He tried to flick it against his thumbnail, but his movements were uncontrollable. I wrapped my hand around his and a few seconds later the match flared to life. Taking the can of miniature hairspray, he brought the match up and sprayed the can.

Whoom!

The aerosol caught fire and shot toward Nurse Shue's face. She brought up her hands to block the fire, but it was no use. Mac stumbled forward, and Nurse Shue screamed in agony and fell the rest of the way to the ground, rolling around. I was about to open the door to the tunnel when I felt that prickling on the back of my brain like I'd been experiencing recently.

Something wasn't right.

The last of the hairspray fizzled out, and Nurse Shue was still on the ground, moaning. Tossing aside the empty can, Mac turned to me and grinned. My eyes went wide at the drool sliding out of his mouth. "Told you. Lots of usth--uthses for hairspray and gum wra—wrap—pers."

I leaned down and hugged him. "Mac, I need you to go upstairs and get help. Get the others out of their rooms and stay together. Call the police. Can you do that for me?"

"What about oo—you?" Mac shook his head. "I thi--thinnnk the drug is takin' hold."

I closed my eyes and felt the pull even harder now. "There's something I have to do."

"No. Gonna th-sthay wit you."

I laid my hands on his shoulders and again tried not to laugh at the absurdity of the situation. Drool was sliding down his mouth, his eyes were half closed, and he was listing to one side...but he was going to stay down here and protect me.

Warmth filled my heart at his brave declaration. I wasn't used to people standing for me and fighting. My mom brought me up to be independent and to fight my own fight. I'd always lived my life that way. Until suddenly here comes this eighty-year-old man who thinks he's a TV superstar, barely able to stand up on his own feet, swearing to protect me.

I gently placed my hands on his shoulders and bent down until our heads touched. "Please don't argue. Trust me.

There's something I need to do. I will be okay. You've taken Nurse Shue out of commission, and I need to finish this up tonight. Go help the others."

Mac blew out a breath, spittle flying everywhere. "Well, I don' like it. But I'llllll go."

He stumbled over to the side of the wall and slowly slid by Nurse Shue. I half expected her to reach out and grab him like you see in the movies...but she didn't. She just laid in a heap on the floor.

"Go!" I cried.

Mac slowly slid his way along the hallway and then dropped down to his hands and knees when he got to the stairs. I felt a weight lift from me as he crawled up the stairs to safety.

I closed my eyes and whispered the only sensing spell I knew by heart. "Hear me now I ask of thee...open my eyes to help me see."

There was a soft rustling in the air, and a cool breeze lifted the ends of my hair off my shoulders. I could hear the whispers getting louder and louder.

Boiler room.

I slowly opened my eyes. Keeping a watch out for Nurse Shue, I waved my hand in front of the boiler room door. The door slid back to reveal a pitch-black room. I cautiously made my way over to the metal door and peeked inside. I couldn't see anything.

With one more look over my shoulder at Nurse Shue, I stepped into the room. I conjured up an energy ball and held it in my hand...partly for the light, partly for the protection. If Nurse Shue came after me, I'd zap her with the energy ball.

198

The room was what I'd expect from a one-hundred-fifty-year-old stone structure. Dirt floor, broken stone walls, and a smell that made me want to lose my lunch.

I caught a glimpse of another door and held up my energy ball as I walked closer. Looking to see where Nurse Shue was, I reached out and touched the door. A shock I'd never experienced ripped through my body, and I stumbled backward. I could sense a presence behind the door.

I waved my hand and pushed the door open. I couldn't see a thing in front of me. The energy ball didn't give off enough light. Knowing I'd have to scramble for a plausible explanation if I got caught, I let the energy ball fizzle out and then threw up a low globe of light—just enough to see about ten feet in front of me. Luckily the glitter globe was a pale white this time, so I had decent exposure.

This room was an expansion of the previous room. It was a standard-sized stone room with a dirt and stone floor. The only thing different was the copper pipes jutting out from the stone walls.

A set of broken, rusted out stairs led to another area of the boiler room...one that was three times bigger than the room I was in. I hurried over to the stairs and looked down. Four huge boilers stood side-by-side together with huge copper pipes again jutting everywhere. My light wasn't strong enough to illuminate what all was down there, and I figured that was a good thing.

I whirled around when I heard a low moan over in the darkened corner of the room I was standing in. I took a tentative step toward the sound, then gasped when I saw Nurse Shue chained to the wall, her emaciated body barely moving with every breath she took. She tried to open her eyes, but it was too much of an effort.

CHAPTER 22

"Wh—what's going on?" I stared, stupefied, at the woman I thought was Nurse Shue, my mind still not able to take in what I was seeing. How long had this person been down here in the dark, cold room?

"Figured it out yet?" Nurse Shue's voice sneered as she shut the door behind her.

I whirled around, and it suddenly all clicked into place. I wasn't staring at Nurse Sandy Shue in the doorframe...I was staring at her crazy twin sister, Nurse *Mandy* Shue. The sister who'd been in the asylum. Now it made sense as to why I couldn't tell if she was lying or not. The answers she gave were true from *her* perspective! Not from Nurse Sandy Shue's perspective.

Mandy swiped the air frantically back and forth with a knife, her body jerking furiously with each move.

Where the heck had she gotten that?

You know how crazy people are! It's always something with them! Yes, it is! Yes, it is!

"Rex," I whispered. "You're okay."

Of course I am. They don't call me Rex the Rebounder for nothing!

Tears slid down my face, and I quickly wiped them away.

Whaddya need me to do? Rex ready and willing!

"Make sure Mac and everyone is safe."

Leave you alone? You sure, Lexi? You sure, kid?

"Yes. See to the others."

I felt a rustle and then smiled as Rex dropped down to the floor and scurried away. Careful to avoid crazy Mandy. But Mandy was too far gone to notice the rat. Between the enormous amount of pain she had to be in with her face and arms burned like they were, plus the whole I'm-the-crazy-delusional-evil-twin thing she had going on...catching a rat was the last thing she was thinking about.

"It wasn't supposed to be like this," Mandy said as she moved closer toward me. "But you just couldn't leave well enough alone, could you?"

"What do you mean?" I stalled for time as I planned my next move.

"Do you know *why* I did all this?"

Because you're crazy?

"No, why?"

I knew I had to lure her away from Sandy chained to the wall. I couldn't risk Sandy seeing me use magic on Mandy when the time came to take her down. With a tentative look over my shoulder, I slowly took a step down the rusted-out stairs.

"I was in love with Dr. Melvin Stark. He was the first person who ever really got me. Who didn't judge me. I looked forward to our sessions every week. I thought he understood my feelings for him. I could tell he wasn't happy at home. He spent so much time here at the asylum."

I reached out and grasped at the rail, careful not to fall backward. I took another step down the stairs.

"One day, I got up the nerve to tell him how I felt about him." Mandy laughed bitterly. "Oh, he was all sorrowful and said the right things. How a relationship between a doctor and patient could never work out. How he was held to a higher standard. Fraternizing with patients and staff wasn't permitted. All the right things."

It always amazed me how cunning insane people were. Their ability to hide the crazy and function in a day-to-day environment. I was the kind of witch who threw up my hands and went back to bed if I was having an off day. I couldn't imagine spending my life hiding and masking my true self from people so perfectly.

"I found the tunnel by accident. I was pacing in front of the windows in the courtyard, watching all the stupid families coming and going one day. I crossed in front of the secret door and noticed a tiny crack. Like it hadn't been shut all the way. I entered the tunnel and heard voices down in the dungeon. That's what we called it back then. That's where they kept the *really* crazy people, you know?"

As opposed to the sane ones like you?

"I tiptoed down the stairs and heard *my* Dr. Stark...*my* lover telling that cow Nurse Hawthorn how much he loved her!"

Mandy screamed the last part at me loud enough to cause her sister to stir. Sandy moaned a little louder from the corner.

"Shut up!" Mandy screamed. "I'm about ready to put you out of your misery in a minute, anyway! So just *shut up!*"

"We can just end it right here," I said. "You give yourself up and get the help you need."

Mandy laughed maniacally. "Do I *look* like I need help? I think I'm perfectly sane. Totally within my rights to be angry at the betrayal I've had."

"Okay," I said, realizing she wanted to talk. Which was fine by me. I still wasn't one hundred percent sure how I was going to take her down without using magic in front of her sister who was still chained to the wall.

"I knew exactly how I'd get my revenge on the good Dr. Melvin Stark. How I'd bring him to his knees." She blinked at me then, as if seeing me for the first time. "Do you *know* how crazy the other people in here were? You could convince them of anything. It wasn't hard to manipulate three or four ladies into seriously believing Dr. Stark had violated them. Just plant the right seeds, repeat the story over and over again until they were convinced it was true, and they blabbed. I had him, and he knew it. The night he died, we had our normal therapy session, and I told him what I'd done. I also told him I knew about him and Nurse Hawthorn, and how I'd let it slip to another aide right before coming down to the session what I saw going on between them." She laughed again, the power of it all making her sound like she was high. "You should have seen the look on his face! He knew I had him! What was he going to say? Yes, he was sleeping with a nurse but not the other women. No. No one would believe that. They'd assume he was sleeping around. Everything he'd worked for was ruined. His practice, his family. Everything. I made sure of it."

She closed her eyes and relished in the victory, and I chose that moment to flee down the steps. I needed to take her deeper into the boiler room to fight her.

"Get back here!" Mandy screamed as she took off after me down the rickety stairs.

204

I hit the bottom of the steps and sprinted for the abandoned boilers. I could hear Mandy breathing heavily behind me. My eyes had adjusted a little better to the darkened room, and I could make out certain items. Abandoned wooden wheelchairs, mangled gurneys, bedpans, and various other antique medical supplies.

I suddenly pivoted and landed in a fighting stance.

"I get why you hurt Dr. Melvin Stark, but what about now? Why come back and kill Nurse Noland and Pauley?"

"It's our twelve-year anniversary, you know?"

"I know. But what does that have to do with Nurse Noland?"

"My stupid sister made it sound all so wonderful the last time she visited me. Like I gave a crap about her life or anyone else's life at this miserable place. She was always going on and on about how she and Nurse Noland were such great friends with Dr. Stark. Of course, she'd never told him about *me*. About how *my* life was torn to shreds here by his father." Mandy cracked her neck and switched the knife to her right hand. "Then during her last visit she bragged about Dr. Stark seeing her best friend, Nurse Noland. And it was like it was happening all over again! That woman was taking the life *I* should have had! She was taking *my* happiness...*my* wonderful life."

Oh, yeah. You and George Bailey have so much in common.

"And then Sandy told me about Paul Ridgeway. I had no idea Officer Ridgeway was a resident here. Not until Sandy went on and on about how happy Dr. Stark was to have him around and in his life after all this time."

Mandy leaped forward and swung the knife at my face. I ducked and she flew by me. I stood and swung around to face her once again.

"So I got the idea to come down here and see for myself what was going on," Mandy said. "I didn't need that stupid job at that stupid nursing home. I told them so. Packed a few things and came back to my old stomping grounds. I waited until the nurse on morning duty was away before sneaking in. If I got caught, I'd just play at being Sandy. No one would know the difference. I've been memorizing her moves for years.

"When did you get here?" I asked. "How long have you been playing at being Sandy?"

Mandy shrugged. "I don't know. Maybe two weeks now? I got here a few days before I killed Nurse Noland. The day I arrived, I stayed in the tunnel until shift change, went to Sandy's room, and waited for her to get off work at midnight. One quick hit to the back of the head and she never knew what hit her. Just like Pauley and Mac."

Now we're getting somewhere. The actual confession, then I could take her down.

"So you brought her down here," I said. "Why? Why keep her alive?"

Mandy shrugged. "I don't know. Insurance. I wasn't sure how it would all play out. I worked out two or three different scenarios in my mind. I'd keep her alive, and if it looked like I wouldn't need her to take the fall, I'd come down and kill her. If it looked like I'd need her, like it does now, I'd drag her back up the tunnel stairs, pin a suicide note to her, admit to killing Nurse Noland out of jealousy, and

206

killing Officer Ridgeway because he had fingered her and it was only a matter of time before someone figured it out."

"You are aware your sister looks like death, right? You've had her chained down here for nearly two weeks. No one in their right mind would believe—"

"Shut up!" Mandy screamed as she swiped the knife through the air.

Crazy suicide plan aside, I had to give it to Mandy. She left her job with no forwarding address, her parents were dead, so there was really no one that would check on her to see where she was. She could totally just assume her sister's life, and no one would ever know that it was really the evil twin that did the killing. Even though a thousand movies and scary stories had been told of such things, no one *really* thinks to finger the other twin.

"I knew I had to break up Nurse Noland and Dr. Stark. Let him feel the pain of that rejection. I told him I caught her with another man. And of course he believed me...he thought I was his trusted friend Sandy. The stupid fool! And that was a great feeling. Until..."

Mandy's voice trailed off and I prepared myself for another attack. I figured she'd just worked herself into another rage and needed to lash out.

And I was right.

With a bellow, Mandy ran straight for me, knife slicing at the air. I decided to take the most dangerous element out of the equation and lifted both arms up in the air. Using my right hand, I blocked the knife from swinging at me, while at the same time using my left hand to knock the knife loose.

I couldn't help the smug look on my face. I knew she wasn't expecting the move. Mandy let out another scream, ducked her head, and barreled straight into my chest.

So much for my superiority.

We both landed on the ground...me on the hard stone surface, Mandy on top of me. Before I could catch my breath, Mandy sat up and straddled my waist and pinned my arms to the ground.

"I'm not finished!" she shouted, spittle flying from her mouth. "Then somehow Nurse Noland figured out something was off. She came to me in my room the night she died. She said she knew something was wrong with me. I told her she was right. Then knocked her out cold."

I tried to struggle and get out of her vise-like grip, but it was no use. I was going to have to think of another plan.

"So I grabbed one of the laundry carts from our upstairs hallway and heaved her inside. At twelve-thirty at night, I wasn't too worried about all the other people being out in the hallway. I carted her down into the tunnel, and in between the first floor and the basement I let her body drop down the stairs so it would look like she fell down the flight of stairs where I placed her. Unfortunately, she didn't die from the fall. So I had no choice but to reach down and snap her neck."

I forgot to breathe. I was seriously staring up into evil. Someone who could speak about taking someone else's life like they were just twisting the lid off a soda bottle.

"Then I hauled her down the dungeon hall and placed her at the end of the stairs. Everyone thought it was an accident. Mainly because I told the police that she'd told me

208

she wasn't feeling well and confessed to me she was going to sneak down to the infirmary and get some medication." She laughed. "The police are so gullible."

I glanced to my right and saw a bedpan about three feet away. If I could concentrate and move it a little closer and wrap my hand around it, I might be able to use it. But before I could focus on sliding the bedpan closer, Mandy jammed her knee into my throat, cutting off my ability to breathe.

"Then Paul Ridgeway had to go and make even more noise than he already had been. Spending the day yelling out it was me. Only these people were too stupid to realize what he was saying."

Spots danced before my eyes, and I quickly conjured up an energy ball. I didn't have full use of my hands to lay her out flat with it, but I flicked it as hard as I could at her stomach. She screamed and rolled off me, the knife falling to the floor. I sat up and was about to go in for the kill shot when I heard shouts above me. I quickly waved my hand in the air, distinguished the light globe, and plunged us into darkness.

Unfortunately, I'd taken my eyes off Mandy when I zapped the light, and once again she was on me like a spider monkey. I fell back and cursed as my head hit the floor. Mandy jumped on top of me again. I could barely make out her outline in the dark.

Pissed and in pain, I bucked my lower half off the ground, wrapped my right leg around her neck and pushed out with my foot, shoving her off me. I reached over and moved the bedpan with my mind, grabbing onto it when it hit my fingertips. I had no idea where she was, but I brought the bedpan over and down as hard as I could. Her grunt let me know I hit my mark.

"Lexi!" Detective Hackett shouted. "Are you down there?"

I coughed and rubbed my throat, easing a little of the pain. "Yeah." My voice sounded hoarse, even to my own ears. I tried again. "Down here."

Beams of light danced in the air above my head before finally landing on me. I could make out myriad other voices. I lifted my hand to shield my eyes and waited for help to arrive.

You okay, Lexi? You hurt?

"Hey, Rex," I whispered. "No. I'm good. Thanks for staying with Mac until help arrived."

No problem! They don't call me Rex the Protector for nothing!

I reached down and ran my hand affectionately over the brave rat.

Dozens of shoes clamored down the metal staircase, and I breathed a sigh of relief that the case was truly over. Never had I wanted to go home so badly.

The good news was, I'd managed to make a clean capture. No need to call in my handler to pick up my mess. That should make the Academy happy.

Gotta go! Gotta go!

"Me, too," I whispered.

"Someone set up some lights down here," Detective Hackett yelled. "You okay, Lexi?"

"Yeah. I got a confession from Nurse—well, actually, from Nurse *Mandy* Shue. This is Sandy's evil and crazy twin sister."

Detective Hackett whistled. "I can see that. You hear of these kinds of things, but you never really experience them."

I snorted. "You do now."

He helped me to my feet. "You sure you're okay?"

"Yeah. How's Sandy up there?"

Detective Hackett shook his head. "Not sure. I got an ambulance coming."

Mandy Shue groaned and then let out a string of curses when she realized what was going on. Two uniformed cops reached down and hauled her to her feet. One read Mandy her rights, while the other patted her down. The curses flying out of her would make a sailor proud.

Detective Hackett guided me over a few feet away from the chaos. "It was dangerous and foolish what you did."

I smiled but said what I knew he wanted me to say. "I know. I should have waited for you to get here."

CHAPTER 23

I sat down on the cold floor in my room, folded my legs close to me, and centered myself. My body and mind were still racing after everything that'd happened. I needed to be focused as much as possible to get myself back to my time.

The ambulance had arrived on scene shortly after a screaming Mandy Shue was hauled away. The paramedics gave Sandy Shue a pretty good chance of survival. She was severely dehydrated, but they had high hopes for her. Dr. Stark insisted on riding in the ambulance with her on the way to the emergency room.

Mac was also attended to, and the consensus was he just needed a few more hours to let the trace amounts of the drug wear off. When the paramedics tried to get him in the ambulance, he adamantly refused to go. Dr. Stark called the graveyard nurse to come in a little early and explained to her what had happened. After ten minutes of answering questions, she'd promised to keep an eye on Mac during the night.

I'd answered all of Detective Hackett's questions, got the other residents back to their rooms, and then realized with a heavy heart that I wouldn't get a chance to say goodbye to Nikki.

When I'd said goodnight to Mac, he grabbed hold of my arm before I could leave. "Something tells me I won't see you in the morning."

Tears filled my eyes, but I blinked them back. "Of course you will."

"Don't kid a kidder," Mac had said. "I only wish you could have met my family. My grandson, he's only a year old, but I can already tell he's going to be just like me...smart, wildly handsome, and a heartbreaker."

"I'm sure he will be." I'd leaned down and gave Mac a hug and a quick kiss on the cheek. Knowing full well I'd never see him again.

Gonna miss ya, kid. Had fun. Had fun.

I opened my eyes and smiled at Rex.

"I had fun, too. I've never had a rat as a familiar before. But I have to say, it was awesome. I couldn't imagine doing this assignment with anyone else."

Safe travels, Lexi. Gotta go! Gotta go!

I smiled as he bolted to the closed door. Chuckled when it took him a few extra wiggles to get his bottom half through the small opening. That was definitely something I'd remember to tell the other witches during our debriefing. My familiar was a rat with a big butt.

Taking my tourmaline necklace out from underneath my Guess sweatshirt, I grasped the stone and breathed deeply. When I felt I was ready to go, I started my spell:

> *"From this time I must depart.*
> *I've done my job and time can restart.*
> *Bring me home, cosmos, I ask of thee.*
> *In my own time is where I need to be."*

***

I opened my eyes and let out a joyous whoop, even though my stomach recoiled and I nearly lost my insides. I was back in my bathroom. I stumbled over to the mirror and was elated to see my long, blonde hair was back to being layered and smooth. Shaking my head, I relished in the feel of the hair swishing over my neck and cheeks.

"Yes!" I cried as I gathered it up in my hands and then let it fall down around my shoulders.

"Yes? As in yes you're ready?" a voice called through the door.

Omigosh! I'd completely forgotten about Shawn!

I quickly stripped off the Z. Cavaricci jeans and rolled them in a wad. "Hey, Shawn, can we talk about tonight?"

"Sure. Through the bathroom door?"

I whipped the Guess sweatshirt off and dropped it on top of the jeans. "I just need one more minute. Zipping up my dress."

I searched frantically for my summer dress. It was exactly where I'd thrown it. I picked it up off the ground, unzipped the back, and slid it over my head, leaving it unzipped for the moment.

Picking up the clothes, I shoved them and the empty box in my one and only tall cabinet where I kept my towels and toiletries.

With one more fluff to my flowing hair, I opened the door and leaned provocatively against it. "About tonight. Could we maybe go somewhere else?"

Shawn looked surprised. "I thought you wanted to go to Gravestone Winery?"

Giving him my most agreeable smile, I turned and presented my unzipped back to him. Lifting my hair up, I rested my chin on my shoulder. "Could you zip me, please?"

214

In truth, I could have waved my hand and zipped it using magic. But I figured this was a better way to go.

"Sure," Shawn said.

I turned back around and felt him fumble for the zipper. A few seconds later the material gathered around my body as he zipped me up. I let my hair fall down around my shoulders and back before turning around.

"The thing is," I said as I ran my fingernail over his cheek and down his throat, "I really don't think I could do Gravestone tonight."

"Why do I get the feeling you're trying to manipulate me?" Shawn asked.

I blinked in surprise and dropped my hand. "What do you mean?"

"I mean we've been dating for a month now, and I've come to pick up on certain things when it comes to you, Lexi Catherine Howe Sanders. When you feel pushed or backed into a corner, you come out swinging. Only it's not always with your fists...sometimes it's like now. With your flirting and sexuality."

I jerked back from him. "I don't know what you mean."

He took a step toward me, grabbed my wrist, and brought it up to his lips. "Yes, you do." He pulled me against him. "The thing is, Lexi. If you don't want to go tonight, you can just tell me. You don't have to play a part for me."

I wanted to rage at him. I wanted to hit him, tell him to leave, to never come back.

But I couldn't. Because he was right. Manipulating men was just something I'd always done. It was easier than actually working things out.

He tilted my chin up to him and looked me in the eye. "Lexi, do you want to go to Gravestone Winery tonight?"

I closed my eyes briefly before swallowing and looking into his hazel eyes. "I actually don't want to go to Gravestone tonight, Shawn."

He grinned and let go of my wrist. "See, that wasn't so hard, was it?"

I curled my lip and rolled my eyes. In truth, it was much harder than I wanted to admit. But before I could process that any further, Shawn turned me until I was backed up against the bathroom wall.

"Now," he nipped playfully at my lips, "where is it you want to go?"

"Hmm?"

Shawn chuckled in my ear, sending shivers over my body. "I asked where'd you like to go tonight?"

"Anywhere but Gravestone," I whispered as I wound my arms behind his head. "Anywhere but there."

I was about to marvel at my luck at finding a guy like Shawn, when my apartment was plunged into darkness.

"I can fix that," we both said at the same time.

I laughed. "Well, I bet I can fix it in a way you've never heard of."

Shawn nipped at my neck one more time. "Oh, yeah? I don't think it will beat my way. I was taught this trick by my Grandpa Mac. He was the smartest man I ever knew. The ladies all loved him, too."

I gasped and my heart skipped a beat. "You had a Grandpa Mac?"

"Yep. Haven't I mentioned him?"

216

"No," I whispered.

"He passed away when I was twelve, but I'll never forget all the things he taught me. In fact, I think for a couple years he lived at the old Gravestone place when it was a nursing home. Then after it closed he got moved to another place in Kansas City."

"H-How? How can you fix it?"

"With a gum wrapper," Shawn said. "Just wrap it around the—"

But I didn't let him finish.

I could feel the tears rolling off my cheeks as I pressed his lips to mine. I wanted to laugh at the way the cosmos worked, but I was too busy relishing in my joy.

****
Hey Reader,
Do you like mystery games? What about a free story? Turn the page for your first clue!

SCAVENGER HUNT!

We're going on a scavenger hunt!

Collect one code word in the back of each of the five Witch in Time Mysteries and unlock bonus content from your favorite time-traveling witches.

Your third code word is: **A**

Good luck!

Dear Reader,

You've followed Lexi Sanders through the hallways of a former insane asylum as she solved her murder--but that's nothing to the perils Mariana Galvin is about to face.

Are you up for the journey?

Pack your bags because we're headed to 1968 Chicago. Mariana must face three of her biggest fears: ghosts, abandoned cemeteries, and an urban legend that may or may not hit a little too close to home for her.

Read Book 4, *Witch After Time*, in the A Witch in Time Mystery Series today!

JENNA ST. JAMES BOOKS

Ryli Sinclair Mystery Series Order

Picture Perfect Murder
Girls' Night Out Murder
Old-Fashioned Murder
Bed, Breakfast, and Murder
Veiled in Murder
Bachelorettes and Bodies
Rings, Veils, and Murder
Last Stop Murder
Gold, Frankincense, and a Merry Murder

Sullivan Sisters Mystery Series Order

Murder on the Vine
Burning Hot Murder
PrePEAR to Die

ABOUT THE AUTHOR

Jenna writes in the genre of cozy/women's literature. Her humorous characters and stories revolve around over-the-top family members, creative murders, and there's always a positive element of the military in her stories. Jenna currently lives in Missouri with her fiancé, step-daughter, Nova Scotia duck tolling retriever dog, Brownie, her tuxedo-cat, Whiskey, and long-haired tortoise, Cleopatra. She is a former court reporter turned educator turned full-time writer. She has a Master's degree in Special Education, and an Education Specialist degree in Curriculum and Instruction. She also spent twelve years in full-time ministry.

When she's not writing, Jenna likes to attend beer and wine tastings, go antiquing, visit craft festivals, and spend time with her family and friends. Check out her website at http://www.jennastjames.com/. Don't forget to sign up for the newsletter so you can keep up with the latest releases! You can also friend request her on Facebook at https://www.facebook.com/jennastjamesauthor/ or catch her on Instagram at http://www.instagram.com/authorjennastjames.

42904310R00136

Made in the USA
Lexington, KY
21 June 2019